Gary E. Gardner

Accidental Accidents

DORRANCE
PUBLISHING CO
EST. 1920
PITTSBURGH, PENNSYLVANIA 15238

Dorrance Publishing Co
585 Alpha Drive
Pittsburgh, PA 15238
Visit our website at *www.dorrancebookstore.com*

ISBN: 978-1-6480-4577-6
eISBN: 978-1-6480-4663-6

1
Warren

Warren Maypoole left work as usual at 5:30. At 6:00 he arrived at home. Walking through the front door he hit the light switches and like every other night for six years, he placed his wallet, badge, keys, and phone on the small bookcase at the entrance to the living room. There was no dog happy to see him when he arrived. Nor cat on the back of the couch. There was no wife to greet him as he strolled through the dining room to the kitchen. At thirty-six, he was a man living alone in a house some have said was much too large for a man like him.

Warren did not believe it was too large. He felt it suited him perfectly. Similar to a Cape Cod but with an addition added four years ago to expand the kitchen and dining room. The three bedrooms and two baths allowed Warren to fill the house with anything he thought would interest him or that would be useful in the future.

Warren didn't think there was a problem; he was not lonely or depressed. He stood at 5'11" with blueish green eyes, and his hair was a light brown. At 170 pounds he was a little light but still looked fit. Clean-shaven, and since he spends little time in the sun, very light skin. Work was good to him, and the friends he had respected his privacy. Unlike other men he had known, Warren had never come home to television and microwave dinners. Also, he believed in a good eight hours of sleep nightly. With a respectable library occupying one of the three bedrooms, there was always, depending on his moods, a good selection of books to read. Books, cooking, and games—they were the three favorite activities in his life. Not the electronic games or video.

Warren dealt with logic, crosswords, chess, anything that would challenge him. One reason he loved going to work was his duties consisted of analyzing data from different sources. He worked for the CIA and the amount of information that comes across his desk is staggering. Most of the time there is random bits coming from different directions, countries, and departments. His job, of course, is to decipher and interpret this sometimes-irrelevant data and somehow make sense from it all. He enjoyed the cryptic messages the most. Sometimes there is no rhyme or reason in the messages. To be able to disseminate this information is why he was given his own office by a window.

His ability to handle complex reports and messages had not gone unnoticed. His other love is cooking. Two freezers were in his utility room: one of vegetables that he had frozen in small bags dated and another with meat prepared the same way. Regardless of the time he returned home, he always found time to cook a nice meal that would impress even the most finicky eater. This was Warren Maypoole's life in Washington DC. It was a happy life as far as he was concerned. Orderly, organized, and quiet. All that was going to change soon.

2

Time for Work

At 8:00 sharp Warren entered the large government building, dodging others entering and exiting. Using his badge, he passed through the electronic turnstile with guards on either side eyeing him suspiciously. For thirteen years he had been passing through this gate. He wondered if they would miss him if he did not show up one morning. Probably not. He made his way to the second floor, heading to his office, nodding and smiling to the men and women at their desks or standing, discussing the day's agenda. After walking to his desk, he turned on his computer and sat back in his chair waiting for the installation of security software. The process usually lasted five minutes or so, which allowed time to make coffee. After he had his coffee, the emails were checked, and it was time to work. Work was relaxing to Warren and no matter how hectic it was in the office he was able to stay focused to work on what he was given. Having his own office afforded him the luxury to close the door that drowned out the normal sounds of a busy office. Today was like any other day working for the company. A beep announced an email was sent for him. A very unexpected one.

3

The Proposal

At 10:00 Warren was standing in front of a door marked "Director Henry Davis" He received an email at a quarter till 10:00 asking him to attend a meeting in fifteen minutes. Rarely has he been invited to the director's office, especially thru email. He raised his hand to knock but hesitated. "Deep breath, Warren," he murmured as he knocked. From behind the door a voice said, "Come," so he did. At the desk sat a man in his fifties with close-cropped hair, almost black and a dark tan. He was dressed in a tailored suit, which fit him perfectly. Davis definitely looked the part. When Davis stood, Warren realized he was much taller than he remembered. At least five inches taller than himself and fifty pounds heavier. Warren glanced around the office and noticed it was surprisingly sparse. Three nice comfortable chairs faced his desk. A large safe, against the wall with two filing cabinets. That was it. A picture of Teddy Roosevelt had the distinction of being the only article on the wall. The director shook Warren's hand and said, "Good to see you. Have a seat."

"Thank you, sir." Warren sat opposite Davis in one of the three chairs. He thought this was a very unusual meeting with the director, but also, he was alone. He began to feel anxious and concerned. Warren has never been insecure while working for the government, but at this moment he felt out of his comfort zone. Davis must have sensed Warren's uneasiness.

"Please, Warren, don't be alarmed. We have a proposition for you. That's all. An opportunity—" He stopped as the door opened. "Ah! Chris, come in. This is the man I was telling you about."

"Mr. Maypoole, pleased to meet you."

"Thank you," he said as he put out his hand to shake.

"Warren, this is Chris Matthews from the logistics department. Chris, here sit down. We were just starting." Warren realized who Matthews was. Dark intelligence. A more accurate description would be dark side. He was built similar to Davis with the same hair and demeanor. He swore they were bred from the same mold.... the CIA—he guessed always did strive for uniformity. The silence was overwhelming. Warren wanted to leave badly.

"Warren, we have a few questions, if you don't mind."

"That's all right, sir."

"Have you ever done any field work?"

"No, I haven't"

"How about weapons?"

"I haven't had any formal training, but I grew up with guns. I had my first rifle at ten. Since then I had a few. Handguns also."

Matthews asked, "Would you be interested in a new position? Temporary, of course. It would be helpful to all of us in the company. We believe you would fit in nicely."

Davis agreed. "Warren, we have been reading your file and are impressed with your work for the past thirteen years. It seems you have been instrumental in breaking numerous messages and your supervisor is very pleased with the reports you create."

"What do you think, Warren?"

Warren was now uncomfortable. He felt as though he was being forced but not forced. The game is to flatter, then move in for the kill. Something like that.

"Can I ask what is involved in the position, sir?"

Davis said, "I'll hand this over to you, Chris."

"I will start by saying that nothing discussed here leaves this room. Agreed?"

"Agreed, sir."

Matthews slid his chair a little closer towards Warren. "As you know there are certain people around the world that are involved in the illegal trade of weapons or drugs. Men or women that operate outside the law with corrupt politicians or very powerful friends. Oftentimes they are a danger to ours or other countries' national security. You deal with these men daily but in a hands-off position. We know where these people are but have no recourse. Frankly, we would like to change that."

"How, sir?"

"In certain cases, we have been able to eliminate the people in question."

"You mean kill?"

"Or dispose of them."

"Okay."

Matthews now looked uncomfortable.

"Warren, we need a way to...." He paused.

"Kill?"

"How about we just say disappear?"

"Okay."

"To kill... without having it appear as though he was actually killed."

Warren interrupted. "Excuse me, sir. Don't you train people for that? Heart attacks, car crashes, and by other means?"

"You're right. We do, and most times it will go unnoticed. There are situations where we have to be discreet and do things so no one would be compromised. The United States cannot afford to be seen as a country that is taking measures to assassinate anyone it feels is unworthy or threatening."

"I understand," Warren said.

"Good. For example, Warren. If there was a man in Parliament who was totally corrupt and everyone in Britain was aware of this. Say one day he gets hit by a car and dies. No one over there would believe it was an accident. Even if it was. Can you see? Without a doubt the British government would be accused of taking him out." Matthews took a breath. "Therein lies the problem."

"How can I help?" Warren asked, still not sure what was expected of him.

Davis said, "You are one of the best analysts we have here. You take random information and somehow are able to see a logical pattern, or better than that you anticipate people's moves that no one else sees. However what interests us more is your uncanny ability to decipher messages and develop games. We need someone to create a situation where an accident occurs with absolutely no trace of foul play. Where no one will question the authorities if they rule it that way. No connection to anyone."

Warren sat back running scenarios through his head. A series of events or a combination of unconnected accidents to create another. To Warren this was to be the game of games. A challenge of a lifetime.

Warren looked at them both and said confidently, "It can be done."

Davis and Matthews were a little surprised. Looking at Warren, they saw he was already making calculations and running the math.

"Very good, then. I'm glad to hear it." The next half hour was spent going over details. Davis stood and offered his hand to Warren. Matthews also. "We will contact you tomorrow to start your training."

Warren Maypoole walked to his office and sat at his computer. He didn't even bother to turn it on. Staring at the blank screen, he wondered what he had gotten himself into. Matthews explained under no circumstances would he carry a weapon. His orders were explicit: if his plans did not succeed, he was to abort the mission and come back to Washington. Warren was not a killer. They all knew that. It was not in his nature. "Oh well," he said out loud.

The next morning, he met with Chris Matthews and another man, Allen Day. Day was to be his handler during his assignment. Responsible for travel, hotels, and any questions Warren might have. He would be Warren's contact. For the next five days they went over how to act and react, safe houses if needed, and communications. That was the extent of his training. Warren was handed his papers, credit cards, and airline tickets and told his reservations were for tomorrow.

"Go home and get some sleep,". Day told him. "You have a long day ahead."

"Yes, sir," Warren replied. He knew he didn't have a chance in hell.

"He doesn't have a chance in hell," Davis told Matthews. They were in the cafeteria on the first floor, sitting far from nosey diners.

Chris sipped his coffee. "Henry, we don't have much to lose, do we? I mean if it all goes to hell or he gets caught.... What in God's name were we thinking?" He paused for a moment. "He has no training at all. A computer geek. Why couldn't you suggest an easier target than Bernelli? There will be guards everywhere at the hotel, and he is not a man to trifle with. A lot of attempts have been made on his life and he is still around."

"I know all that, Chris. Listen, if Warren fails, we will deny everything about the assignment but even if he fails, we can learn a lot. He is a good man, but he is clearly out of his depth. The data he will be sending us may be beneficial to us in the future. I suspect all we get in return from this operation are his theories."

Chris still was not convinced. "I hope whatever happens we can keep it from prying eyes."

"Don't worry. Let's see what he comes up with."

"Still, Maypoole has no idea what he's up against."

"True," Davis said, "but this is going to be interesting."

Chris got up to leave. "By the way, do you have a monitor?"

"Shelly will be there. No contact. She's there just to watch."

"All right. See you tomorrow, Henry."

4

First Assignment

Warren was on his way to Miami. His first time, and he was excited. Sunshine, beaches, and cold drinks. He knew he was sent there to work, but a little fun may not be that bad. The three-hour flight allowed him time to study the file Allen Day gave to him before he left Washington.

Mr. Dominic Bernelli was sixty-two, married with no children. His home is in Rome, but he travels frequently. Job related. He was one of the most notorious gun runners in the world. They say he is the owner of a distribution business that deals in legitimate goods, but his money certainly came from weapons smuggled to the Middle East and Asia. Warren has spent a lot of time through the years intercepting messages to and from Bernelli, but he has always been behind a desk. Now he will see firsthand how he operates. Warren didn't understand why he was untouchable, but he guessed that would be clear once he met the man.

Once the plane landed, he found his bags, and took a cab to the hotel. The Hotel Armada was one of the most prestigious hotels in Miami. It was amazing to walk through the lobby with its marble floors and walls. The ceiling was forty-feet high. Ten-foot chandeliers hung gracefully with hundreds of lights that gave the room a warm and inviting glow. People were everywhere heading in one direction or another. There were porters and concierges keeping order throughout. Warren marveled at the efficiency and wondered if this was a normal day for them.

At the end of the lobby, he could see the restaurant that, in his estimation, held close to 200 guests. The seating was not overly congested. You could tell they spent time designing the layout.

The bar was at the very end, L-shaped and the large entrance allowed all guests to move freely in and out.

At one end of the bar was the exit to the pool. On the opposite side of the bar was a souvenir shop, but in Warrens eyes it was more like a department store. He walked to the elevator and got off at the third floor.

His room was only four doors away so one minute later the door opened, and a porter showed him in. The size of the room almost took his breath away. Never in his life had he seen anything so… extravagant. They went room to room, and Warren tipped the man before he left. He knew he would never be able to afford a room like this. Once in a lifetime luxury. He was grateful for the experience.

Warren found the small bar and wine rack and poured himself a glass of red wine and helped himself to the snack tray on the small dining table. Compliments of the company. After finishing the glass and not wanting to forget why he was there, he decided to go down and visit the shop and pool. Elevator down, turn right, and straight out the door. The signage was remarkably easy to follow, and in no time, he was at the pool area. He realized then he was completely out of his depth. He looked at his clothes. New shirt and shorts, $100 shoes—he looked good, but these people looked great. *So, this is what money does for you*, he thought.

He walked to the side where the bar was, sat, and ordered a glass of wine. Studying the people around the pool, he was fascinated by how the rich live. The pool had to be over a hundred feet long and maybe fifty feet wide. Lounge chairs lined the sides with towels and umbrellas if needed. A woman pushed a cart around the pool filled with towels, lotion and whatever one might need while at the pool. The bar, where he was sitting, seated at least thirty, plus there were tables close by. Another interesting part of this, he thought, was very few people were actually in the water. Maybe they swam at the beach. It was right out front of the hotel. While he was enjoying his thoughts, he noticed a woman about halfway down the bar. Very pretty, he thought. Long brown hair below her shoulders, very blue eyes, and a blue blouse. She was not paying any attention, of course. Women usually do not, and he was here to work, not to play. There was something familiar about her, though. He couldn't pin it down. Like him, she didn't seem to fit. Almost out of place.

5

Scouting

A large tent was on the other side of the bar. It was a while later he discovered it was for massages. They accepted reservations to have your massage right at the pool. Very convenient. Not far from where Warren was sitting was a large statue that looked as though it was made of concrete. An old Roman or Greek God from the looks of the dress and helmet on its head. Had to be at least twenty-five feet tall and was tilted towards the bar. He had to assume it was heavy. It was only supported by one brace by the walkway and no one seemed to notice it at all. A very unusual statue at a beach.

Warren spent the next hour sipping his wine, observing the people, and enjoying the scenery. Most of the guests at the pool were women and all were competing for the best and smallest bathing suit. He was secretly judging all the contenders. Thanking the bartender, he got up to wander a little. He needed more information. That meant he had to know the hotel inside and out. He walked to the bar inside the restaurant, through the lobby, and even the restrooms. He rode the elevator to all ten floors checking the hallways on each one. Then he made it back to the restaurant to order dinner.

The woman in blue watched as Warren ate his dinner. She waited until she was convinced he would be there for a while. She took the elevator to the third floor and walked to Warren Maypoole's room. With a master key, she let herself in. She was looking for the file Warren had on Bernelli. Mostly his notes he had been making since he arrived at the hotel. She knew he did not have them on him, so they were somewhere in this room. He was a novice in this business, so she didn't anticipate any difficulties. It was not in the room. She searched everywhere. Mattresses, rugs, chairs, in his drawers. Nothing. She went as far as looking in the air vents. She decided to return another time. The room was as it should be, she thought, so she locked the door and went down the hall to her room. Taking off her shoes, she opened a beer and made a call to her boss.

Warren loved to eat, loved to cook, but this was as good as it gets. He ordered a twelve-ounce steak. Potatoes, green beans, corn on the cob, and a salad just for fun. Dessert was not far behind. Anyone watching would not pay any intention to the man sitting alone eating enough for two. He was content eating and listening to the music in the background. Although he looked uninterested, he was aware of his surroundings and of the movements of the guests. The woman in blue, when he first sat down to eat was watching him. He saw her leave moments later. Curious. he thought. It took him at least an hour to finish, but to him it was worth it.

Once in his room, he felt as if something was different. Nothing tangible, but he sensed it. He saw nothing out of place. Still, something was different. He worked until eleven o'clock writing his notes before he undressed and climbed into bed and thought of the woman in blue.

The woman in blue put the phone down, lay on the bed and stretched her legs. She could not understand why the file was not in Maypoole's room. She was sure she searched everywhere. In the morning she decided she would double her efforts even if the room needed to be torn apart. So much for subtlety. She closed her eyes and fell fast asleep thinking of the man down the hall.

6

The Hunt is On

The alarm woke Warren up at 7:00 a.m. He jumped in the shower, shaved put on a new set of clothes. He wore a beige shirt with white shorts. He was happy with the colors. He was learning to fit in with the guests quite nicely. By 7:45 he was having eggs and sausage with a full pot of coffee. Halfway thru his coffee he spotted the woman in blue. Today she had on a yellow blouse with white shorts and looked much better than yesterday. She sat with her back towards him, but he knew she was conscious of him. Warren finished his coffee and made his way through the lobby out to the beach. He made it a point to pass close enough to the woman for her to notice. He grabbed himself a chair and relaxed in the sun. The day started off perfect. Full stomach and sunshine were what he needed now. Later on, he would begin his search for Bernelli.

The woman in blue, now yellow, entered Warren's room determined to find the file. She started in the kitchen area and was working her way to the living room. She stopped as she walked in. There was the file, laying on the table by the couch. She looked around expecting to find him in the room laughing at her. These were the notes from yesterday that he must have written last night. Why would he leave them out on the table? He is untrained but this is careless. She read through his notes and was amazed how detailed they were. There were calculations, measurements, drawings, and statistics. How many men and women were at the pool and how many were in the pool. He had counted how many were seated at the bar by the pool and in the hotel. Distances from the pool to the restaurant, to the lobby and from there to each elevator. She admitted she was flabbergasted how he could of possibly compiled all that data and information after one night. In fact, she followed him the whole time and he never gave any indication he was actually paying attention. She photographed as much as she could then hurried back to her room. She had to call her boss to tell him what she found.

Warren figured he had spent enough time on the beach, so he decided to try the pool again. As he approached the entrance, a man in a straw hat carrying a newspaper passed by. That's him. Warren said almost too loud to be heard by the others around him. Warren turned to get a better view. That has to be him. Warren stayed on his trail.

Mr. Dominic Bernelli removed his hat and robe before he entered the tent for a massage at the pool. He was tired and needed to relax. His wife suggested he try one this morning as he did not sleep well the night before. Sleep did not come easy to Bernelli. His business occupied much of his time. Perhaps a massage would do him good. He felt his muscles being worked hard but not uncomfortably. He slowly drifted to sleep. An hour later, he woke feeling well rested.

"That was needed," he told the man. "Tomorrow at eleven o'clock."

"Yes, sir" was the reply.

Warren lost the man in the hat. When he tried to be so inconspicuous, he became reckless. This he thought was a consequence of not being trained properly. He needed to find Bernelli and study his movements, but this was not working. Matthews and Davis allowed him five days to come up with a plan. That was it.

He asked himself. How many people die in hotels? Not many. What accident could possibly occur in a hotel. He had to learn as much as possible about this man Bernelli no matter what it takes and soon. Or, maybe he should just reconsider his decision and go home.

Sitting in the lobby seemed sensible to Warren because sooner or later Bernelli will have to pass by. Another hour should do it, he thought. Then he saw him. He was with his wife walking through the lobby hand in hand on their way to the bar. They took two bar seats and ordered drinks. Warren slid in a booth at the end of the bar to watch. The couple sipped their drinks talking and laughing.

The woman now in yellow also sat at the bar. She had followed Bernelli and his wife to the bar and found a seat. She noticed Warren at the other end. How did he know Bernelli would be here? The funny thing was he paid absolutely no attention to them. He was looking in the other direction. Bernelli saw Warren and asked if he would like a drink.

Warren raised his coffee and replied, "Just this, sir. Thank you."

Bernelli laughed and said, "I know too early," turned, and continued talking to his wife.

Warren had seen the woman in yellow but decided not to acknowledge the fact. When the man in the hat left, he did the same.

She watched him leave but didn't know why. He passed right by Bernelli and didn't even look at him. She stayed for another two hours, keeping an eye on him and his wife. They had drinks and then some more.

She had seen Warren and Bernelli speak to each other. She couldn't hear, but it seemed pleasant enough. What was he doing? They said he was a computer whiz; he deciphers codes as an analyst, so maybe he is onto something she doesn't see.

Warren followed the couple to the restaurant which worked out well for him. He was hungrier than he realized. He sat a good distance apart, but they were still in his sight, so he was able to have his lunch. He was running the day's events over in his mind. What exactly did he know about this man? He had a room on the top floor, liked to drink, as did his wife. His moves were predictable. Breakfast, lunch, bar pool then the bar again. He had very little interaction with the other guests and no phone calls. For Warren this could be easy or next to impossible. He would learn more, but for now he left the happy couple alone and went to his room to work on his notes.

He was right. The lady in yellow was in his room. The file was left on the table for her to find easily enough, and she read through the notes entirely. Before Warren left this morning, he fastened thin transparent strips of tape on the pages, and when turned they would be released. He used the tape at work sometimes to see if anyone came in his office. His notes were detailed with the calculations and drawings but gave little information about his subject or plans. They along with whatever conclusions or ideas were removed and placed elsewhere. That would keep her guessing for a while. She was working for either Davis or Matthews for sure. He should have known they would not risk sending him alone on such an assignment. The next couple hours were spent working on his notes. He took a much-needed nap, then worked for four more. Tomorrow would be a better day for him. He made it to bed and slept through the night.

7

The Game

The woman in yellow now wore red, and she was on her phone in the lobby, talking fast and seemed pretty agitated with whoever was on the other end. Warren intentionally walked close by for her to see him. He could see her watching him as he went to the front entrance, exited, and came back in. He picked up the lobby phone spoke a few sentences, hung up then went to get breakfast. He was sure she was getting all of it. Good. this was going to be a long day for her.

Warren had his breakfast of eggs and sausage again. His two cups of coffee were good. The man in the hat had not come to breakfast yet, unless he was here earlier so Warren would have to search for him.

Passing by the woman in red, he noticed she had only toast and coffee and was eating slowly. Probably the phone call he surmised. She is going to have to get up now to see what he's up to.

The woman in red was not happy. For twenty minutes she was on the phone with her boss and the only thing she accomplished was she lost her appetite. Three days since she arrived in Miami and had little to show for it. Yes, she had Warren's notes copied and though they were detailed, they were missing, she was sure, important information. She knew they were incomplete. Her boss wanted more than she could get. He suggested she find the missing files; if not they could send someone else to find them. That part did not go over well.

"I'll get them," she said and hung up on him. She was still upset a half hour later when Warren walked past her. *What is it with him?* she asked herself. He is so calm, almost happy to be here. He walks around without a care in the world knowing he on a time schedule to cause someone to die. Why did he go out to the beach, come back in a few minutes, then stop to phone someone? Who did he call? Where is he now?

She had to find out soon or lose her job. How hard can it be to keep up with an amateur? Of course, she is capable. Why would her boss question her? Then again how is it she has no idea what Warren is trying to do. It looks like he's following the wrong man. Maybe it's some game he is playing with Bernelli. Or her?

Perhaps he left the file out in his room for her benefit. If so, why was it incomplete? The lack of training means Warren is unpredictable. His movements are hard to explain. He is bound to fail. She was convinced of it. She finished her toast, downed her coffee, and forced herself to her feet. One way or another she was determined to, one, find Warren, two, find Bernelli and three, bring this to some conclusion and get back to Washington. The lady in red was now on her way to the pool to find Warren.

It was 10:30 and Warren was at the bar alongside the pool. It was too early to drink, so he nursed a soda instead. He had mapped out the entire pool area and was convinced this was the only possible place to have an accident. He had the clear view of the pool and let his gaze wander from one side to the next. He calculated, eighty percent of the pool were women, which seemed high, but he didn't normally frequent many pools, especially pools like this, so he had nothing to base his findings on. Fifteen percent of that number were in the pool swimming. The twenty percent left were men, and there were none in the water. All sat around or stood at the bar, and Warren assumed they were watching the eighty percent of women.

A bald man waited outside the massage tent and looking at his watch Warren supposed he was in line for the 11:00 appointment. The woman in red walked by him smiling. He had been waiting for her to show. Her mood was better, and she found a chair near the end of the pool and put up her feet.

10:50. The man in the hat sat with his wife five feet from where Warren was sitting. They were at a small table with an umbrella and already had their drinks in hand. At 10:58 the flap on the tent rose and a small tan woman popped out. She smiled at the bald man waiting in line. The man removed his robe and entered the tent.

The woman in red saw Bernelli go into the tent. She also saw Warren's gaze follow him until the tents flap closed. "He does know," she whispered. He has something planned. At exactly 11:00, Warren stood and walked to the side of the pool. Something or someone had his attention, but she couldn't make out what. She moved a few chairs down because of the sun. There she saw him standing at the end with his back turned. What happened next was astounding and shocking. At the time she couldn't comprehend, but later on it would become clear.

From her vantage point she could clearly see Warren standing by the pool close to the entrance to the hotel. No one noticed as he bent to examine the support of the statue and the surrounding area. He stood and turned around at the same time a woman came out of the pool and fell into him. Warren held on to her, his arm around her waist. Both smiled and a few words were exchanged. The walkway was only three feet wide, so people had to brush against them to get by. Another woman with one of the large carts carrying towels was trying to pass, so Warren and the woman separated and as she did, she glanced back to smile again. The woman in red laughed at the sight of these two flirting. Afterall, he was young and could appreciate bathing suits.

Warren tried to move out of the way from the cart but a man, about three hundred pounds at the same time shoved his way past. He knocked Warren a few steps backward and pushed the cart off the walk into the grass and cursed the poor girl for being there. When Warren backed up, more guests were trying to get out of the way. Everyone's attention was now focused on the cart and the fat man yelling. The man in the hat came over to help but the cart had, with the man's weight behind it, slammed into the support of the statue. There was a loud crash. Suddenly everyone was up and running as the statue was tilting even more than it was originally. The statue slowly came down and when it was almost on Warren, he dove to get out of its way. While Warren was in the air, he hit the man in the hat and his wife along with another man. All four hit the ground hard and rolled to the side to avoid the statue. It crashed to the ground, pieces broke off and were lying everywhere. Warren helped them to their feet, the man in the hat grabbed his hand and shook over and over.

"Damn, mister, that was something else. You just saved our lives. Can't thank you enough, I'll tell you, son, that was incredible. That statue had us until you jumped in front of it. Are you all right? By the way, my name is William Shelton. From Toledo. This is my wife Charlotte. Warren was still shaken and a little overwhelmed." Then it hit him.

"What did you say your name was?"

"William, Shelton. We owe you a large drink after that."

"Oh Christ," Warren said a little too loud. I was after the wrong man.

William asked, "Son, are you all right?"

"Yes. I'm all right just a little shaken, that's all."

"Good, I am glad to hear it. I'm going to take Charlotte to our room for a while. I'll look for you later."

More people were crowding around, then Warren heard screaming.

"What was that?" William asked.

They looked towards the bar and to the side, the statue they all just noticed, landed on the massage tent. The tent was flattened. They saw employees trying to help those inside the tent and security keeping the crowd at a distance. A woman close to Warren had her hands over her mouth, looked at them, and said, stuttering, "They found someone inside. He was dead."

Charlotte cried, "Oh my."

"Who was he? Do you know?" asked William.

"They say his name is Bernelli. I've never seen him around. Have you?" They all shook their head no.

"It's such a shame. He was in there for a massage, and it collapsed."

Warren almost collapsed himself after hearing Bernelli's name. They watched the efforts by the employees for a few more minutes.

"Damn shame," William said softly. "What are the chances? Well, I'm off to our room. I'll see you later for that drink."

Ambulances were now arriving. The police were questioning everyone. All of a sudden, the pool became a very busy place. Warren left and sat at a table at the bar in the hotel. The guests were all talking about the accident.

William was right. What are the chances? Warren ordered a double scotch. No rocks.

The lady in red sat and was watching the crowd walking around in a daze. Some were crying, not because they knew Bernelli, but they all saw the statue hit the tent. They also saw a brave man save three of their other guests. The noise was deafening. the police were trying their best to piece together the best they could how this occurred. It was going to be a long day at the Armada Hotel that was for sure. There were cameramen everywhere, and she needed to leave. She needed a drink.

8

Regrouping

Warren saw her first as she rounded the corner. She stopped when she spotted him, hesitated for a moment, then asked if she could join him.

Warren said, "Of course." He could use company now.

"Hold on a second," she said. She went to the bar, then came back with a drink in her hand.

"Scotch?" he asked.

"Oh yes."

He raised his glass. "The same."

"Interesting day," she said. The lady in red smiled. Warren thought she had a nice smile.

"My name is Warren."

"Yes, I know. I'm Shelly. Are you all right? You took quite a tumble."

"Yes. I'm fine. I may be a little sore tomorrow, but... I'm okay. Do you work for Matthews?"

"Yes, I have worked for him for a few years now."

"I thought so. It was his party from the beginning."

Shelly was looking at him. She studied his features. He had a strong face and was good-looking close up. A soft voice but very clear. He was noticeably shaken but was still in control. Under the circumstances it was understandable.

"When did you know?"

"The first day, at the bar by the pool."

"Seriously?"

"Yes."

"How? There was no way you could have known that the first day."

"We both looked the part, but it wasn't really us."

"That's it?"

"Yes. After watching for a while, plus, I confirmed it later when I realized you were looking for the file."

"Then why did you leave the file out?"

"I didn't want you tearing my room apart. Also, I wanted you in the game."

"In the game. This was not a game, Warren. Far from it. You could have gotten yourself killed. You knew who Bernelli was."

"You were there; I was safe."

"That's a hell of a gamble."

"Not at all. I was fine here. No one knew who I was. I was not suspected at all and would not have been."

"Why did you want me in the game, as you say?"

"If I would have said something, they would have called you back. I liked our little back and forth. It was fun. Almost like foreplay. I was hoping for it to last longer, though."

Shelly's eyes widened.

"I'm sorry. That wasn't proper."

She was thinking Warren is nothing like his profile. He was so incredibly observant, focused yet he has this playful attitude and personality.

"It was frustrating at times trying to figure you out, but it was fun," she whispered. Shelly was blushing; so was Warren. "I had a feeling you were being too obvious."

Forty-five minutes passed, and they were still talking and laughing.

She went to the bar and brought back two more scotches. Both doubles.

"I needed this she admitted. What a day."

Warren agreed with her. "When do they expect us back?"

"I'm not sure; maybe tomorrow or the next. Depends on what they say after I make the call. By the way. You never called Allen Day to check in."

"I didn't need anything. I was fine. I figured you were reporting in. There was nothing for me to add."

"You are a strange one, Warren Maypoole."

"That I am." He reached for her hands and held them. Shelly felt the warmth flow through her; she almost pulled away. He looked into her eyes. The very blue eyes. He let go of her hands, and she placed them on her lap. That was close, she thought. He made her feel normal and comfortable. It must be the alcohol, she decided.

Warren was enjoying her company.

When Warren started laughing, Shelly asked, "What is so funny?"

"I was just thinking. How could you possibly explain to Matthews how this happened?"

She burst out laughing. She had to put her hand over her mouth to quiet herself.

She knew he was playing with her, but she didn't care. Bernelli was gone, and she was having a good time.

The waiter brought over two more drinks. Warren said, "That was nice we didn't even ask."

"I guess we look like we need them," Shelly replied.

They both sat quietly with their own thoughts. Warren wanted to spend more time here with her but was not sure how to arrange it.

"Shelly?"

"Yes."

"I have a question." Warren looked serious.

"All right. Ask away."

"Spend the night with me?"

Shelly was not expecting this from Warren. He was looking at her waiting for a response or reaction.

She also was not expecting what came from her.

Finally, she said, "I will."

9
Shelly

The next morning, they were both up at 8:00 a.m. Shelly called Matthews and told him she would be in sometime this evening. Matthews was very pleased with the outcome of the assignment. He and Davis were watching the videos on the news and reviewing police reports. At this point they were still a little mystified how Warren pulled this off. The police were satisfied it was an accident. Rumor was that throughout the underworld, they agreed with the findings. He would see them both sometime tomorrow.

Warren was happy this morning. They were eating breakfast, talking about what Matthews had to say.

Shelly sat at the table in one of the hotels big fluffy white robes. He sat looking at her. She felt his stare.

"What?"

"You're beautiful."

Shelly blushed. "Shush." She got up from the table and gave him a kiss. "I'm going to shower. You finish your report."

He could not believe he had the courage to ask Shelly to spend the night. He was thrilled he did. She's intelligent and beautiful. He found her to be passionate and loving. She was tall, close to 5 10 , slim but worked out often for strength. She had the long brown hair with just the right amount of wave to give her style. Her blue eyes were what you would see first when meeting.

Warren did think she was beautiful. As awkward as he is around women, Shelly made him feel comfortable. When they decided to go to Warren's room to spend the night, they didn't realize it was only 2:00 in the afternoon. They went to his room and dove into the bed. Later they ordered dinner and a bottle of wine. After dinner they sat and had their wine and talked. When he mentioned bed, they raced to the bedroom. Sometime that night they fell asleep.

Warren didn't know how to explain yesterday to Shelly. Most of what occurred was intended. All the notes show what was planned, to a point anyway. He couldn't confess to her about following the wrong man. How could he make that mistake? All except that he could be honest with her. Shelly was out of the shower and lay next to him on the couch. The couch was large enough so they could both lie down without turning on their side. Warren held her close. She put her arms around him to snuggle.

"You know, Warren, this is an impossible relationship. The government does not condone fraternization with other agents."

"I am aware of that," Warren said. He could see no way around it. "But this is nice, and I would like to remember you this way. Anyway, we will find out more when we get to Washington. Changing the subject. Would you like to talk about Bernelli?"

"You know I do. It's been driving me crazy, but you need to answer a question first."

"What's that?"

"Where did you hide the file the first day?"

"Oh, the time you broke into my room."

She giggled and said yes. Warren looked at her and said, "In my room. It was there."

"I looked everywhere."

"I put it by the door."

"There was nothing th—she got up on one elbow and growled. "The tray."

"Right. I put there on my way out."

She put her face in the cushion. "I'm so embarrassed."

"Don't be. You had no way of knowing the maid wasn't coming that day. She had already been there, and I was still eating, so, she left."

Shelly said, "Okay. She pulled him up to a sitting position. Now start."

"Where?"

"At the beginning." She kissed him.

Warren knew he would have to do this. A dress rehearsal for Davis and Matthews.

10

The Explanation

"When I first arrived and had a chance to walk the hotel, my assess-ment was that it would be impossible."

"Why was that?"

"First off Matthews chose the worst location he could for an assignment like this. Think about this. How many accidents happen in hotels that cause death? None that I know of. Second, the hotel being closed off from the world, exclusive, means guests will stay within the boundaries of the hotel. That's why they chose a place like this. There isn't much to work with. What could happen? Seriously. An air conditioner falls from a window. A toaster in the bath or a fall from a balcony? All this would be suspect to anyone in-vestigating." Warren took a breath and paused.

Shelly watched the change come over him as he spoke. From playful and funny to serious and self-assured. The analyst in him was coming out.

"The next day I realized the only thing constant were the guests. Their movement and their personalities. In order to design a plan, the guests had to be involved. unknowingly of course. The set up."

Warren knew this part was true. All this was in notes.

To Shelly he said, "Most people are predictable when put in a situation that causes fear or confusion. If you're on a crowded street and a car hits a pole close by, what do the people on the sidewalk do? They will scatter. You can even predict which way they will run or jump. It is the same at the pool, if you block a path people will try to get around some way. At a hotel like the Armada, where the people have money and are entitled, inconvenience is not tolerated. They respond the same but with a little more attitude. The woman I held at the pool; her experience told her that a man will always come to her aid. No question. Although I did hold her longer. Thankfully she didn't mind. That three-hundred-pound man was not going to let us stand in his way. His response was appropriate for him to push by that hard to show his anger and impatience. We were guests so he would not be rude or inconsiderate. He took it on the girl with the cart and pushed as hard as he could. I had to rely on people acting as themselves in order for anything to be accomplished. It was a calculated risk. An educated guess."

Shelly asked about Bernelli.

"Bernelli had an 11:00 reservation for a massage. He would be there for an hour."

Warren had seen the man waiting by the tent before 11:00. He saw him enter the tent.

"I had an hour to put something in motion."

"So, the statue was part of the plan?"

"Yes, it was essential," he admitted. "It had to be. The statue was leaning and propped up by a single support close to the walkway."

"I don't know, Warren. How could you set that up? You could not know."

"You're right, Shelly. I couldn't. All I could do is start something and let nature run its course. There is no way I could guarantee it would work. You were there. What are the chances?" He could tell Shelly was trying hard to make sense of it. All of it was true, just the wrong man.

"All right, so you were going to stand there creating a roadblock hoping someone would come by and knock the statue over?"

Warren looked at her. "The girl with the cart passes by every fifteen minutes. It's thirty inches wide and weighs about seventy pounds full. When I held the woman at the pool, the cart was still fifteen feet away. That's why I held her so long. I was waiting. I also saw the fat man. I just hoped something would work."

"What would you have done if the fat man was polite?"

"Probably pushed him into the cart," Warren smiled.

"You know this isn't over. I can't process it all now. How am I going to explain this to Matthews?"

"I have no idea."

Shelly asked a few more questions, then changed the subject. They sat for an hour discussing tomorrow's meeting with Matthews and Davis and how they would go about seeing each other when they get back to Washington. They exchanged phone numbers to stay in contact once home.

"I still can't believe I asked you to stay with me. I have never been so forward with a woman."

"The assignment must have been good for you," she added. "I am even more surprised I accepted. I, let me think, have not been on a date for about six months and that one did not end well from what I remember. Warren, you know we have to be careful. Right?"

"Yes, I do."

"This is not an office fling. We're in the field, and the field has different rules and is subject to more oversight. Understand?"

He nodded.

"Good, now kiss me so I can go to my room and pack."

11

The Debriefing

Shelly and Warren took the elevator to the lobby where she checked out. The man at the desk apologized for the tragic accident that occurred at the pool and hoped it was not responsible for her leaving. She assured him it was not. She needed to return to Washington for work. The hotel offered two free nights for compensation, at any time. Shelly smiled and said she was very grateful; she would return soon.

"I will miss you," Warren said as he kissed her.

"I'll miss you too."

"When you go to your debriefing, be careful with Davis and Matthews. Your new at this, Warren. They have been around a long time. This is what they do." She hopped in a cab and left for the airport wondering if they would see each other again. Shelly felt sadness for the first time in years. "Damn," she whispered. "How did this happen?"

Warren felt he owed a visit to William Shelton to have that drink. He found them at the bar enjoying their last day at the hotel.

"Hi, buddy, you made it." Shelton was smiling and having a great time.

"Yes. My shoulder was sore from that fall yesterday."

"That's okay. Let me get you a drink. That sure was a mess at the pool. I feel bad for that poor man. We are thankful you were around when all hell broke loose. Charlotte here was just telling me he was a big man in Italy. Owned a business somewhere in Rome. His wife left this morning to go home, and they said the body would be shipped this week. By the way, what's your name in case anyone asks for you for an interview? We were proud to mention you when the reporters showed up."

Warren was caught off guard. Reporters... he couldn't be seen on camera.

"Brian Wilcox. From Pennsylvania." It was the first name that came to him.

"Pleased to meet you. Charlotte, this is Brian."

Warren thought she had a little too much alcohol this morning. "Hi, Brian," she almost spilled her drink as she turned to him.

William and Charlotte were nice people from Toledo, but Warren wanted to pack and get out. He said his goodbyes to them and headed straight for the elevators. He had to make sure the media was not in the hotel when he was leaving.

The flight home seemed longer, and most of the time Warren was thinking of Shelly. He missed her being around the hotel and missed her more from their last night together. He did not want to accept that their relationship would end before it got started, but now the meeting with Davis and Matthews tomorrow was important, and he knew they would question everything.

He would have to convince them that it was designed for that outcome. His notes should confirm his story. Shelly's testimony along with his should be sufficient.

Warren did not want to lie to any of them, but the mistake with Bernelli was too much. Especially if he wanted to keep his job at the company. It weighed heavy on his mind. Fortunately, he was the only one who knew the truth. He would have to continue with his original story. By the time he arrived at his house he was exhausted and most likely would have slept until the next evening if the phone had not woken him.

Allen Day wanted to know what time he would be at work. He grudgingly said in an hour and hung the phone up.

The effects of the flight and lack of sleep were taking its toll on Warren. He made it on time to the meeting, but Davis must have noticed he was not himself. Warren walked in the office to start the debriefing.

Davis asked, "How do you feel, Warren?" Davis was at his usual place at his desk. Matthews was to his right side, and Day was across from Matthews.

"Moving a little slow, sir."

"This will be quick, then you can go home and get some rest. Allen will be with us during the debriefing, if you don't mind."

"No, sir, that's fine." Not that his opinion would matter, he thought.

Warren sat between Day and Matthews, he was trying to look professional, but he didn't believe it was going well.

Allen Day was unlike the other two in every way. Shorter, twenty years their junior and not dressed nearly as well.

After Day started questioning Warren, he realized why Day was here. He was very articulate and astute. His questions were to the point, clear, and concise. Warren was surprised at how Day could speak so quickly, listen to the answers, and still write in his notebook.

An hour and a half later, Day ended his debriefing and told Matthews he was finished.

"Well, Warren. I know this was difficult for you, but it was necessary. We wanted to get your story before it was too late. The memory is funny like that. The longer we wait... it's in the details. You know?" Davis wanted Warren to know this was routine with all assets.

"I understand. I don't mind."

"Good, good. Go home and catch up on your sleep. We will talk later."

"Thank you, sir. I am not used to traveling like this." He stood up to leave. Matthews stopped him. Oh God, he thought. What now?

"I have a question for you."

"Sir?"

"How did you make Steiner so quickly?"

"Who?"

"Shelly, Shelly Steiner."

"Oh, sorry, I didn't know her name. To be honest, and in her defense, I was not there to find someone and just get rid of them. I had to formulate some kind of plan with very little resources, and I had to rely on the guests and employees to help with this plan. While there, I observed them all, actually counted them. I saw everyone as an accomplice and studied their manners and personalities. Agents normally do not do that because they are familiar with whom they're looking for. I noticed she did not fit. No one else would have thought twice. I was using what knowledge I had to analyze the guests, to see how they acted. I know that sounds strange in a way, but under other circumstances I wouldn't have been looking."

"So, she did nothing wrong as far as you know?"

"I don't believe she did." Warren was uncomfortable with this questioning, should he defend Shelly too much.

"I had never been in the field. For some reason it didn't occur to me there was someone else. It was naïve, I admit. It wasn't until I saw her that it hit me. Of course, there would be someone out there monitoring the situation. I felt a little better knowing that."

"Well said, Warren," Matthews responded. "You can go now."

Warren was gone.

12

The Debriefings Brief

When the door closed Henry Davis breathed out. "Whew. That was interesting."

Allen agreed.

"Henry," Chris Matthews asked. "What do you think?"

Not sure. It's quite remarkable if you think how it was done. Do you believe it was planned? How about you, Allen?"

"It is plausible. We have all read the report and his notes Shelly brought back with her. It is very detailed and is spelled out the day before. Shelly verified it was not written after the fact. So, it was planned at least on paper."

"How do we know for sure, Allen?" Henry asked.

"Listen, Henry. Shelly was at the pool and confirmed everything. We saw the video some of the guests recorded; we have eyewitness accounts. Christ, he even saved three people from getting crushed. Anyway, Maypoole is not your typical agent in the field. He is naive and awkward as hell but as we saw, he is resourceful and clever. Though he is definitely out of his depth. However, saying that, we can benefit from his skills."

"My opinion, we cannot train him as an agent," Chris threw in.

"What do you mean, Chris?" Henry asked.

"He may pick up bad habits and lose his edge. We need him to stay Warren in order for him to be effective."

"Allen?" Henry was looking for help.

"Maypoole was right. Miami, the Armada was the most inappropriate place for an assignment. He looked at this logically. Surprisingly he pushed forward and came up with results. He could have said no."

Henry was getting defensive. "We had no idea what he was capable of. We never really expected results."

"I know, Henry, I'm just saying we will have to do better in selecting a place for him where the possibility of an accident being successful is better."

Henry was surprised in the direction this was headed. "You two have already decided to send him out again?"

"I think we should. It worked once." Matthews was grinning.

"Chris," Henry said, "what are you suggesting we do?"

Allen was curious also. "Yes, do tell."

"All right, I have the perfect place in mind. Have you ever heard of a man named Rene Bolon?"

Both nodded their heads yes.

"Information crossed my desk last week. Ironically Maypoole actually discovered it. Bolon is an avid fly fisherman and he spends a lot of his free time in rivers around Europe and the United States. Well, we happen to know he will be in Washington State for two weeks relaxing and fishing."

"Seriously?" Henry spat out.

"We have Warren to thank for getting us the details. He intercepted some messages and sent them up the chain. The Chateau is in the mountains far west, near Idaho. Two weeks, Henry. What do you think?"

"I think that it's perfect. What about you, Allen?"

"Let's try it. Very convenient for us. Be a shame to pass it up."

"Allen, can you arrange everything?"

Chris went on. "There is not a country out there, unofficially of course, that wouldn't love to see Bolon disappear. He will not be missed. And yes, Henry. We will deny everything if it goes bad. Most of all, I do want to see what Maypoole can do with more resources."

Allen was excited. "I can handle the logistics, but I need someone with him."

"In what way?"

"The last time Warren used his real name. Won't work. Also, he was alone in a large and exclusive hotel. He lucked out and didn't look out of place. He needs to be given a chance to work, and he needs to be able to mingle comfortably with the guests. I hate to say this, but we may need to protect him. He is a computer guy but as we saw at the pool, he is not afraid to get close."

"What do you need, Allen?" Chris asked.

"Preferably a woman."

"Why do you say that?"

"Chris, It's a giant hotel in the middle of the mountains. You cannot expect two men to be roaming the hotel and not be noticed. Can you?"

"No, you're right. So, who?"

"Your girl, Shelly."

"She would love that." Chris laughed out loud.

"He needs a wife. She already knows him, so why not?"

"Anyway," Allen continued. "Shelly can handle herself and him if he gets too friendly."

"I can't picture Maypoole with women in the field. Give him a notebook, and he will be fine."

"Allen, you take care of Warren and the paperwork. I will deal with Shelly."

13

The Chateau

Shelly Steiner had her meeting with Matthews early. He handed her the file on Rene Bolon and explained what they needed from her.

"Do you think this is a good idea sending Warren out so soon?"

"We spoke to him and he had no reservations. He agreed with the idea of you coming along. A single man there would attract attention, but he will need his space, so let him do what he does best. Keep him on track and focused. We know he likes his games; your job is to make sure they are not too complicated. Keep his feet on the ground.

"I know this is sudden Shelly, but right now we have a chance to get to Bolon, and we would be foolish not to jump on it. He has friends in high places, so we can't take him out like some regular criminal. We would like to. That's easy. We need this to be clean. If you are not comfortable with his plan tell him to change it. Allen Day will be handling this, so keep him apprised. Be careful with Bolon. He will have bodyguards, and they are very good. Keep Warren away from them."

Warren's meeting was slightly different than Shelly's. Davis was being gentle and cautious, afraid, how he would react this soon after Miami. Warren was fine with going into the field again. Emotionally and mentally Warren was fit. Better than expected. His orders were simple. Make something work. Okay.

Allen Day gave them their travel papers, along with the new IDs. Mr. and Mrs. Fredrick Crawley. They reside in Pittsburg, PA. They are spending the next couple weeks celebrating their fifth anniversary. They will arrive in Washington, tomorrow late and will have to take a car to the Chateau. Warren made the comment that they chose terrible names. Day ignored him.

Warren and Shelly were excited and a little surprised when they heard they were working together.

Away from prying eyes, they could have their secret romance, and pretending to be married would make it easier.

It was late when they arrived at the Chateau—4:00 in the morning. Warren didn't remember anything the porter showed them when they finally got to their room. He and Shelly found the bedroom and were asleep immediately.

Warren was up first. He was showered and shaved and out the door ordering from the restaurant before Shelly crawled out of bed. He was gone an hour before he came back through the door. Shelly was waiting for the food.

"Why didn't you just call room service?" Shelly asked.

"I wanted to take a quick look around. It's a fabulous place."

Warren grabbed his notebook and started writing.

He brought a tray for three, having learned about Shelly's appetite. How she could put so much food down, he couldn't understand. So, he let her eat while he wrote.

"I'm glad you brought extra. I was starving." He sat watching her eat. She noticed, and with her mouth full she said, "What?"

"Nothing. I like watching."

"Be quiet." She laughed.

After completing four pages, he looked over to Shelly still working on a second plate of eggs and bacon.

Warren had his eggs and toast. Although it was nearing 3:00 in the afternoon, breakfast sounded a lot better than lunch.

After knocking off a pot of coffee, life was finally coming to them.

"Warren, how do you have so much to write? You were only gone an hour."

"I know, but I got a chance to do a little investigating. The first floor is huge. It's a hell of a layout."

Shelly got up from the table, went through her briefcase and pulled out a few sheets of 8x11blank paper.

"Here, draw for me so I can get an idea of the layout. You always seem to see more than I do."

She marveled at how he remembered the smallest of details. She'd always thought she was observant until meeting him.

"Show me what you see."

With a pencil Warren started drawing, outlining the first floor.

"Here is the main entrance, the one we came in. This is where the desk is located off to the side. Couches and chairs are here. Restrooms are down this small hall, only about ten feet. The fireplace, you have to see the fireplace, Shelly. You can roast a whole cow in there."

"Warren, please."

"You can, it's huge. Anyway, elevators are against this wall. There are only three floors, but the building is very long. Rooms start past the restaurant here and go for about two hundred feet."

"What is this?" Shelly was pointing to a room off the bar.

"That's a coffee-slash-hangout place with a smaller fireplace. The bar's over in this corner. Great bar. We can go later if you want.

"Conference rooms are at the end of this hall. Only one way in. All the other rooms have multiple openings.

"The rear exit to the river is just past the bar with a huge patio. From there you can go to the river or follow the trails. Stables are on this side."

"They have stables?"

"Yes, they have about twenty horses. We will be concentrating right here." Warren put his finger on the river.

"Why out there, Warren?"

"My experience in Miami taught me, you need room to work with. What better place to have an accident than in the woods? The river should be our best bet. The Chateau cannot control nature. So, tonight we eat, drink, and jump in bed. Not necessarily in that order."

"You already have a plan. don't you?"

"Not quite, but I am working on it."

"She got up to kiss him. What's first."

"Let's go down to have that drink. I want to show you off."

"That's sweet of you."

"I think you're beautiful. Everyone should know."

Shelly showered and dressed and the two made their way into the lobby. The lobby was just as Warren described it. It was amazing. It was not like Miami, with hundreds of people running around. This was quiet, a few guests were lounging by the fireplace and a couple on the chairs reading or on their phones.

There was no hustle and bustle, just people enjoying themselves. She put her arm through his and said, "This is how I want to live, Warren."

"With me?"

Shelly didn't answer. She just smiled.

At the bar, wine and cheese were brought to the table. Shelly was admiring her surroundings. Very rustic. All wood floors, walls and ceilings. The lighting was perfect, and there were wonderful paintings throughout. The taxidermist must have made a fortune. Animals everywhere. She'd never seen so many dead fish in one place before. The restaurant they passed was as beautiful as this. She scanned the area trying to see what Warren would see but soon admitted she couldn't. She could see Warrens eyes studying everyone and everything. He would stop occasionally to soak in something, then continue. All the while talking and joking around as if not a care in the world. She didn't mind not being the center of his attention. He was working. She would have him later. That's all that mattered. She was happy to be with him.

Warren all of a sudden got serious. "Shelly, call Day. Now."

"Why? What is it?"

"Ask him why he has someone tailing us. Don't let him lie."

Shelly called Day's number. The phone rang once, Day picked up.

"Day here," he answered.

"This is Shelly."

"Is everything all right? What's wrong?"

"You sent someone to follow us. Why?"

"Shelly, come on."

"Don't lie to me, Allen. Warren made him."

"How did he—"

"So, you did."

"Yes but—"

"Don't 'but' me, Allen. Send him home now. If you and Matthews do not trust me, then pull me too. I will not play this game. We do not need a distraction with all that is at stake. Got it?"

"All right," Day said. "You had better send some good reports."

She hung up on him. "Jesus, I can't believe they would do that."

Warren put his finger to his lips and pointed to the end of the bar.

She didn't know what to look for, and then she saw it. A man sitting alone, answered his phone, listened for a moment, then got up and left the bar.

"Was that him?"

"That was him, all right. You were great on the phone. You're very pretty when you're mad."

"I'm not mad, I'm pissed."

"I know. You know Bolon is a dangerous man. They wanted you and I to be safe. I don't think they were spying on us."

"You're right, Warren. I'll call Matthews in the morning and apologize. How did you spot him?"

"He was alone looking bored and impatient. How can you be bored here?"

"I bet you he is pissed now. Day will be pissed too. He got made the first day."

"Let's not think about work anymore, all right. Let's drink some more and go to bed. I miss you."

14

A Trip in the Woods

Shelly called Matthews early to apologize for her behavior with Allen Day. She knew they were only sent there because of the concern for their safety. She assured him they would be careful and call if there were problems. Warren was picking up breakfast. By the time he returned, she had already showered and was hungry. They took their time eating, planning the day.

Warren said, "Today will be easy, Shelly. We have all day to walk some trails and visit the river. The weather is supposed to be perfect for outdoor activities."

The Chateau was built on a hill, overlooking a vast forest that extended for miles in all directions. One road leads up to it and when the winter snow comes it is almost inaccessible. That is the appeal of this stone and log building. If you could afford to be a guest here, being snowed in is not a concern. Although there are no winter activities such as skiing or sledding, the idea of staying in a remote area attracts people from around the globe.

Horseback riding is a favorite for the guests. Hiking is popular with its miles of trails and scenery, but fly-fishing is what the Chateau's most famous for and sections of the river are reserved a year in advance. The river is within walking distance, is well stocked, and in areas only three to four feet deep.

For that reason, Warren is paying it close attention. Not because he is a fisherman, but Rene Bolon is a fanatic when it comes to fly-fishing.

He and Shelly left the Chateau through the rear exit overlooking the river, then turned to where the trails began. Signs were posted on the different trails for either hiking or horseback riding, and they found that they had a choice on what distance was preferred. Warren chose the shortest one. 1.3 miles. They held hands to keep up appearances, but also, they have had little chance to spend time enjoying themselves outside of the hotel. The forest was immense, and the trail followed the curvature of the hills up and around without much physical difficulty. They walked slowly, talking softly, knowing sound travels in the trees. About a mile in the walk Shelly noticed he was looking at his watch.

"What's the matter, Warren?"

"Nothing, I was just timing the walk."

"Oh, really. I thought you were happy being with me."

Warren smiled. "I am happy. I wish we could stay like this."

"I'm glad," she responded. "I could stay like this forever." Shelly regretted what she said the moment it came out. Not that it wasn't true, but agents could not allow feelings to complicate matters.

Changing the subject, she asked him about the timing.

"The distance to and from the Chateau, to the river and back again. Also, any of the outbuildings, like the stables, maintenance garages, and anything else around. We need to have as much data as we can get. Even if it turns out to be irrelevant."

He gave Shelly a long kiss and said, "Yes, I could stay like this forever."

She took a deep breath. She knew she was in trouble.

Warren's file had shown that he has few friends and even fewer girlfriends. Basically, a loner. His hobbies are mostly mental, that included books, games, and computers. All she had to do was watch over him.

She has the training and experience. For some reason it felt the roles have been switched, and he was now watching over her. He is incredibly thorough and detailed. Considering his lack of experience, he shows an exceptional air of confidence while working. And... she fell for him.

They walked for another ten minutes, then the forest ended. A large field stretched all the way to the Chateau, down to the river and over to the stables.

They made their way towards the river until they were close enough to see four men, two on the bank of the river. Warren assumed they were Bolon's bodyguards. One stood waist high in water, twenty yards from the bank. The fourth was Bolon, and he was standing halfway across the river. He was casting his rod effortlessly. Warren gave him credit; he was very good. Shelly and Warren walked hand and hand fifty yards off the bank, upriver towards the Chateau which was only a hundred yards from where they were. When they passed by the Chateau the river widened and made a small turn. At the bend Shelly saw a dam filled with uprooted trees, logs and debris.

"What is it, Warren?"

"Beavers. Must be a lot of them."

"Wow, I've never seen one before. It's huge. Are they always that big?"

"No, not at all. They are usually in smaller slow-moving rivers. This one is old. It's backed up a hundred feet or more. Look at the water how the force of the current is keeping the logs in place."

Shelly stood and admired the work of the beavers. "It is amazing," she said.

Warren pulled on her hand, moving quickly, in the direction they just came from.

"What? Where we going?" She had to run to keep up.

"Come on. We're going horseback riding."

"You're kidding, right. We have work to do."

Laughing, Warren pulled harder. "We have time. Can you ride?"

"It's been a while, but, yes."

"Good. The stables are around the corner."

She was trying to keep up. "What has gotten into you? Did you see something out there?"

"Riding will be a nice break for us. Anyway, we can cover more distance on the back of a horse."

At the stables, Warren left Shelly at the gate, then disappeared behind the barn. A few minutes later he showed up with two horses in tow. "Here's yours," he said, handing her the reins. "I was told she is very gentle."

Warren picked up some grain to feed a mule, standing beside a fence. The mule gently ate from his hand.

"Look at you," Shelly said. "You have a friend."

Warren found an apple and handed it to the mule. "He likes it. I wasn't sure. I know horses like them, but this is a mule."

Warren jumped on the horse and galloped away.

Shelly climbed on and saw Warren already racing away. She kicked the horse and chased after him.

"Hey," she yelled, "wait for me."

Warren slowed. "Sorry she's a little frisky."

"Frisky, huh? You think you can get away that easily?"

"Wouldn't think of it."

"I hope not." She pulled alongside and slapped him in the head. "That will teach you."

They rode quietly together, glad to have time alone.

Shelly wanted to talk but understood Warren's need to think. He had this serious look about him.

He did have a lot on his mind, but not all of it concerned work. Even after only three weeks, he felt he was falling in love and believed she was as well. What can he do? Working for the government sure is complicating his life. Thirteen years there and it never occurred to him it was a problem until now.

"You know," he said, "I do not think Fredrick and Louise Crawley sounds right. They should have asked us what we thought before printing the IDs."

"That's what you have been thinking about all this time? I've been quiet so you could work."

"Don't you agree? We could have come up with better names. I do not look like a Fredrick. You definitely are no Louise."

"I don't think it matters, Warren."

"Warren and Shelly Maypoole have a better ring to it." Shelly's heart stopped. She had no idea how to answer.

"What are you thinking, Warren?"

"Matthews and Davis, I'm sure know of our relationship. It's a question of time, that's all, when they bring us in."

"Why do you think that?" She had been expecting a call herself.

"We work for the government and no matter how careful we are, they will know."

They pulled off to the side of the trail. Warren asked, "How long can this last?"

"I don't know," she answered. "I wondered myself. Warren. Let's go back to our room. We will finish this later."

"All right."

They followed the trail to the stables, then walked to their room. Inside, they kissed passionately. and never had that discussion.

15

Reviewing the Data

For hours. excuses were made for not going back to the conversation. Room service was used for the first time, and Warren ordered double knowing Shelly's appetite. He was always amazed at the amount of food she could put down.

Warren worked on his notes, more figures and diagrams. He spent two hours studying the layout, inside and out. Shelly was content eating and writing her own report for Allen Day. He had called earlier wanting an update, so she described some of Bolon's habits and routines. She through in some of Warren's theories to keep him happy. With dinner, came wine. They drank two glasses, turned on some music and Shelly asked Warren what he had written.

"Before I answer, tell me what you remember. I'll fill in the blanks."

"Let me see. Pausing. The chateau is a ten-minute walk to the river. The trail was 1.3 miles and took us maybe twenty minutes. Bolon has three bodyguards with him at all times. He reserves that section from 7:00 until 10:00."

"How wide is the river at that spot?"

She thought for a minute. "A hundred yards, give or take. Downriver, there are rocks and a small bend and upriver is the dam that we stopped to admire."

"And... horseback riding was fun." Both laughed.

"Yes, it was fun. Anyway, that's about it."

"No, it can't be. You scribbled in that book of yours for two hours."

"What I wrote was mostly details. Everything you described was true."

"But...," she stammered. "You wanted to leave. What did you see differently?"

"Nothing. I wanted to be with you," he admitted.

"Oh! That is sweet of you."

"We will have plenty of time tomorrow to work on a plan. I need to get close to Bolon at the river, so I'll go out early."

"Until then...." He kissed her softly.

"Yes...?"

"Come with me." They ran to the bedroom.

When Shelly left the bedroom, she saw Warren at the table. He looked troubled. "Warren what is it?"

"I was thinking, how many bodyguards does a man like Bolon usually have? I mean when they travel."

"It depends. I guess two or three. Sometimes more if they are in an unknown place. Why?"

"When Bolon is at the river, there are three. If I were an international drug dealer, I would not have all my men in one area. That's me of course, I'm not, but I would have one watching from a distance."

"Do you think there is one in the Chateau?"

"I would bet on it."

"How do we find him?"

"Get dressed; we'll go to the bar and find her."

"Wait. What do you mean her? Why a woman?"

"I would have a woman. A woman can go in a lot more places and do things that men cannot. Generally speaking. We have to find her."

They dressed, Shelly in a yellow dress. Her hair was up, and she was wearing a light sweater. She definitely could outshine most of the female guests.

Warren, on the other hand tried to his best but always seemed to fail when it came to fashion. Light pants and a blue shirt with tan loafers were all he could manage.

Walking arm and arm, Warren thought they looked good, but he knew the guests were looking at Shelly who was all smiles.

They sat at the bar eyeing the guests. Five women seated alone, and four men were also at the bar. "How do we narrow it down, Warren?" she quietly asked him.

"Look, Shelly, when I start talking to these women, play along. don't act surprised or awkward."

Shelly gave him a not so nice gaze. "I am the one who is trained, re-member?"

"I know, and you are wonderful."

"Just so you know."

"When I start speaking to one, give me a minute and them come to me."

"All right." Shelly had no idea what he was up to and why was he acting mysterious.

Warren waited until the bartender was at the other end, and he slipped next to a dark-haired woman. He noticed a ring on her finger, made his ex-cuses and went to sit with Shelly.

"What happened?"

"She was married. It wouldn't be her."

Another woman without a ring had a glass of scotch. he moved on.

"Do you know what you are doing, Warren?"

"Give me time."

Warren finished his wine and sat with his empty glass.

"Do you want another one?"

"Not now. Here she is."

Shelly turned to see a tall woman with light hair, a dark jacket over a light green blouse and a dark skirt.

"How do you know?"

"One minute, okay?"

The bartender was missing, and Warren took his empty glass and stood beside the woman. Warren looked impatient, sliding his glass back and forth.

In French, he said, "I have no patience with bartenders here. In France, everyone understands a man and his wine."

The woman responded in French. "I agree. In France we love our wine and our men."

Warren smiled. "And our women."

You speak beautiful French. "You are American?"

Shelly saw them talking, so she finished her drink and walked over to them.

As she stood there, she realized she could not understand a word of what was being said.

"Yes, I am living in Pittsburg, PA, But I had my internship in France. You are from the north are you not? Your accent."

"Yes, I am."

Shelly stood behind Warren a little annoyed. "Hello."

Warren turned to her. "Hi."

In English he said, "This my wife Louise. I'm sorry, I don't know your name."

"My name is Claudette. Nice to meet you Louise."

"I'm Fredrick."

"Your husband speaks wonderful French. Perhaps you should move to France, you would love it there."

"I would like to," Shelly said. "Work does not allow too much travel. We were lucky to arrange this."

The bartender came up and asked what they would like.

Claudette and Warren laughed. "Three wines, please." Warren paid the man.

In French, Warren said, "Claudette, it was nice meeting you. We are going to sit outside."

Claudette responded in French also. "In this Chateau, it is nice to find someone who can speak and drink like French men and look good."

Warren smiled at her. "Thank you. You made my day."

Shelly said goodbye, they walked out to the patio.

Claudette smiled. "A very jealous woman, but she is in love," she said to no one. "Oh well, I guess it's my profession."

Shelly slapped Warrens arm. "What do you call that?"

"What!"

"I cannot believe you were flirting with that woman. In French."

"Damn, Shelly. I was only trying to be friendly. Once she was made, I had to convince her we were who I said we were."

"Are you sure you are the same man in your profile?"

"Yes. That is what they say."

"You could have picked that woman up in no time. That is not in your file."

"You can't believe everything."

Shelly was not smiling. "You speak French?"

"Yes, apparently very good, according to Claudette. You're jealous, aren't you?"

"No, I'm not." She was hiding her face with her hand.

"Look at you. Anyway, that helped out. She would never suspect us."

"You did that intentionally, didn't you? You knew how I would react."

"I was hoping you would be obvious enough to convince her. I'm sorry. We needed to know for sure. Now we know we have to be careful around her while Bolon is fishing tomorrow."

"You are not off the hook."

"Even if I said I love you." Shelly looked at him. He always looks through her, into her. As if he sees something, she doesn't know about herself.

"Even."

"Let's go to the room. I have to rethink certain ideas I had."

It took a about a half hour of smoothing before Shelly calmed down. She was angrier at being jealous than when he was flirting with Claudette. Warren was playing the woman, and Shelly knew it, but it made her realize Warren was important to her. That bothered her. She was weakened, and she should be stronger.

She wanted to resist and be stronger, but she failed.

Shelly lay down with Warren's arms around her and felt safe and loved.

16

The Accident

The alarm woke them both at 7:30. Warren dressed quickly and went to the restaurant for breakfast. When he returned, Shelly had the coffee ready for him at the table and was speaking to Allen Day on the phone. She put the phone down and slid a plate in front of her. Warren only had a small plate of eggs and toast, looked at his watch, and told Shelly he would be back soon.

She showered, had another cup of coffee, and sat looking out the window. She saw Warren casually strolling to the river where the dam was located. When Warren approached the dam, he turned and climbed onto the logs behind the dam itself. He was lying on his stomach with field glasses watching Bolon in the river. She grabbed her glasses from her case and waited.

From Warren's position he could see Bolon clearly. The same two were on the bank and the other in the water twenty yards from Bolon. The dam was solidly built, but the trees and debris made it difficult to move around. A half an hour passed and still no movement from any of them. He had developed a tentative plan this morning and was now trying to put it in motion. The dam was essential to make anything work to everyone's satisfaction.

Warren was so busy concentrating on the men downriver he never heard or saw that he had company.

He felt the vibration first, then a knocking sound coming from the bank. He jumped up with a start.

There was a mule attempting to join him on the dam.

"What the hell?" he said as the mule closed in on him.

He stood looking around for someone or anyone.

"Where did you come from?" he asked the mule. It walked closer to the center of the dam, and Warren could feel the trees move. How the mule kept its, balance he didn't understand, but he needed to get it off. Warren did not want to attract attention, so he tried to push the mule backwards. Then he attempted to pull, curse, and threaten, anything. Nothing seemed to work, so he pushed one more time and gave up. He got off as quickly as he could, looked at the mule, shrugged, and walked straight to the Chateau. Once in, he used the lobby phone to contact the stables about the mule. He hung the phone up when they asked his name.

Walking to the elevators, he saw Claudette sitting in the restaurant. She smiled and waved to him as he climbed into the elevator going up.

Shelly was still at the window with her glasses watching the river when Warren walked into the room.

"What did you do, Warren?"

"With what?"

"The donkey."

"It's a mule."

"All right, the mule. Why did you leave it?"

"I called the stables, and they said they would take care of it."

"What is he doing there? That was your friend, right? The same one."

"I have no idea."

They both had their glasses trained on the dam, a truck pulled up, and two men climbed out. They carefully tested the trees behind the dam with their feet and slowly stepped onto it. When they reached the mule, a man on each side grabbed hold of its mane and pulled. When that failed, they tried bribing it with food. That didn't seem to work out well either. The mule was getting agitated, its feet were moving faster, the men backed off a little fearing something drastic was about to happen. From the window, it looked as though they were calling it to come to them. The only response from the mule was to kick a little harder at the trees trapped behind the dam.

The two men jumped off the dam onto the bank of the river, knowing it was much safer for them away from the panicking mule. The trees under the mule were starting to separate, and each time the mule kicked harder. The men were at a loss at how to resolve this and at this point all they could do is stand and watch. One of the mule's legs became trapped between some of the logs and panic set in. He started to thrash wildly, his head moving from side to side. He began to make frightening sounds that shook the men. It fell on its side and was half in the water; it was still kicking at the logs, anything to get away. The river's current that had trapped the trees was adding pressure on the dam.

The men could see how there were now small openings in the dam itself and the water was finding its way through. With the mule throwing and snapping its head forced the trees apart and the mule fell into the water. There was an eerie sound from the dam as branches and trees started to come apart. Using its legs to push the trees apart, the mule was slowly making the dam unstable. Piece by piece after all these years, the force of the logs and trees, along with the water was tearing it apart.

All at once there was a long swooshing sound and the dam gave way. The water rushed through, pushing the trees and debris down the river. The speed increased the farther downriver it went. The men fishing just below were unaware of the danger headed their way. It wasn't until the sound of the rushing water fifty yards from them attracted their attention. The two bodyguards on the bank were screaming for them to hurry, but there was too much distance to cover to escape the onslaught. Bolon dropped his rod as the first tree hit him. His age and lack of strength would not allow him to hold on. He was dragged under the water and carried away.

The bodyguard was stronger; he jumped on a tree between branches and held on, trying to ride it out, but farther downriver he crashed into the rocks and died instantly.

A crowd gathered outside on the patio, horrified by what they were witnessing. The surviving bodyguards were searching downriver for their employer. It was over a half hour before the ambulances arrived. Two bodies were found, they did not survive, and were identified by the bodyguards. Later the mule was seen walking to the stable. Somehow, he did survive.

They saw Claudette walking from the river. She came up to them. She was crying.

Shelly hugged her. "Claudette, are you all right?"

"Yes. A terrible accident."

"Was he related to you?"

"No, my employer, but I liked him. He will be missed."

"What will you do now?"

"I will go home to France. There is nothing I can do here. I'll be all right. You and your husband take care. Bye, my friend." She spoke in French and made it sound much sadder.

Warren and Shelly were amongst the crowd gathered outside and when the police came to interview any witnesses. It was then time for them to slip away unnoticed. Even though it was only 11:00, drinks were available at the bar. Sitting back in one of the booths, they listened to guests describe the tragedy.

Most were not aware of Bolon's history, nonetheless, he was a guest, and his death was felt by many.

Warren and Shelly sipped their drinks, quietly taking in the events.

"I cannot believe you were on that dam with a mule. That was the most insane thing I ever saw you do. Warren, there is no way you planned that."

"You're right. I didn't."

"Are you serious? The mule was an accident."

"I calculated everything. From the beginning, I knew the dam had to be what caused the accident, so I went there to loosen what I could and to find a way to set it all in motion. I had a number of ideas and was trying to narrow it down, when the mule came. It must have been the same one that we saw at the stables. No one would ever believe this story."

"How were you able to get the mule on to the dam?"

"He did that on his own. At first, I didn't want him there, he was attracting too much attention. When I realized he was not moving, I thought, this is an interesting predicament, maybe he is part of the solution."

"You fed him at the stable. Did you think of it then?"

"Not at the time, but that might be why he followed me onto the dam, looking for another apple. When I couldn't get him to move, I called the stable to make sure someone else was involved instead of me."

"So, you knew it would break up?"

"Not exactly. I hoped it would. I figured if there were others on the dam the mule would panic and the possibility of it caving were good."

"What do you want me to tell Matthews?"

"The same as Miami. It is all guesswork and luck. All I can do is create a situation and hope all involved play their part. An accidental accident."

"Why do you call it that?"

"That's what it is. It was a series of mistakes and blunders that create the first accident. Granted, I plan it and set it up, but I can't guarantee it will work. People and… animals are predictable, but sometimes they will be braver than usual or turn and run. Sometimes it's an accident that all the work I do actually is successful."

"Accidental Accidents. I get it," Shelly said. "It makes sense. Then why did you do all that work drawing and measuring if you knew it would come down to the dam?"

"I wanted it to be the dam. The most obvious answer to our problem is sometimes the best. However, there are so many variables that I couldn't count on it. Outside of the dam. other possibilities were available to us. We just didn't need them."

"You know, sometimes I don't know if you know more than what you say."

17

The Aftermath

As with Miami, there was nothing to indicate foul play. Over a hundred guests witnessed the dam bursting and the two unfortunate men who lost their lives. Rene Bolon was the only fisherman out that morning and he and his friend paid dearly. Also, as Warren's friend William Shelton once said… "What are the chances?" Shelly had to laugh at one comment from the police, there will be no charges filed against the mule.

"Warren, I have to call Allen Day. I'll be back."

When the call ended, she sat down again.

"What did he have to say?"

"He and Matthews heard the news, and they were going over to speak to Davis. He wanted me to tell you good work." Shelly smiled.

"Yes, good work," Warren said. "I should thank you."

"Why me? You're the one who braved the waters and the mule on the river."

"You are always with me, encouraging me to be the best I can be. You are patient when I need you to be. I couldn't do this without you, but most of all because you love me."

Shelly thought she hadn't heard correctly. "I what?"

"You love me," he answered. "I know you do. I love you so much right now. I am so proud to work with you, and to spend our days and nights together."

"Warren!" She was completely at a loss as to what to say. "We work for the government. What do think is going to happen when they find out?"

"I will probably be out of a job."

"Why you?"

"You are important to them. I'm temporary, you know that. All this has been too easy up to now. Sooner or later I will either get caught or someone will get hurt."

"Don't say that."

"Maybe not, but people cannot continue to die from accidents. Others will be curious and look for answers. Davis and Matthews will shut it down."

"You seem sure of this, Warren. How long do you think we have?"

"I would say two or three more, after that, way too obvious. So, does that mean you do?"

"Do what?"

"Love me. Tell me you do. You would make me very happy."

Of course, she loved him, and has for a while, but to admit it.... All right, I love you."

"Now it really doesn't matter what they say or do." Warren was beaming. "All's well in the world."

"You are a strange man, Warren Maypoole."

"I know, but it's all right."

"I am tired, Warren. Can we leave?"

"Yes, let's go. I will order lunch to the room. This assignment is over."

18

Home

The day of Bolon's demise turned out better than expected. After a few drinks, steak, and more drinks, they spent the remainder of the day and night in their room. Mr. and Mrs. Fredrick Crawley checked out of the Chateau at 9:30 the next morning and after a layover in Chicago, they finally arrived in Washington DC around 9:30 p.m. They parted at the airport with plans to meet later when they were settled.

Spending three hours with Matthews, Davis, and Allen Day was more than Warren could handle. They were positively giddy, using every adjective known in describing what they thought of the process and the end result. Warren was tired, he wanted to go home to rest.

Shelly's debriefing lasted as long as Warren's. Davis was concerned about future assignments and wondered if Warren could continue to be effective. Shelly admitted Warren was still not comfortable in certain situations but was dealing with it well. He did need time she believed, before another operation was considered.

"I believe he is worried he will lose his sense of normalcy and his identity."

Allen Day agreed. "He needs his friends and some time in his office before we go any further."

Shelly drove to Warren's house later that afternoon. He had already set the table with an early dinner. Pork roast, potatoes, vegetables, a nice salad, and French bread. As soon as she sat at the table, she attacked the salad.

"I am so hungry. They kept me in that office for hours. Thank you for feeding me. This is excellent."

"I'm glad you like it."

"A man that cooks this good is worth keeping around. That's impressive. I thought bachelors only ate mac and cheese and frozen dinners?"

"No! not this man. When all else falls apart, cooking brings it together. It has a calming effect and also attracts women."

Shelly threw a piece of bread at him. "Don't get cocky, mister." She was impressed at the way he kept the house. For the size, it was very clean and orderly. The furniture was well placed, and he had a lot of books. The dinner, she thought was spectacular. She chased it down with a glass of good wine and was officially full and content. He even washed the dishes. That clinched it, she was hooked.

They moved to the couch and went over their debriefing. Warren said he thought it went well, but when people praise a little too much and smile, it makes him nervous. "Davis and Matthews seem decent enough, but they are politicians. It comes with the job. I try to be careful when I am around them."

"Would it be all right if I stay the night, Warren?"

"I would like that. What about Matthews?"

"Like you said, 'they have to know.' I just wonder when we are going to hear it from them." She held his hands. "I don't know what to do."

"Well, we will worry about that later. For now, we take advantage of our time alone."

Shelly's phone rang at 8:00 the next morning. They had only been up for fifteen minutes with the first cup of coffee.

Shelly, this is Allen. Matthews wants to see you this morning around 11:00. Is that all right?"

"That's fine, Allen. I'll see you then."

"Good. Can you put Warren on?"

Shelly put her hand over the phone and whispered, "Oh! Christ."

Warren looked at her. "What?"

She handed him the phone.

"Hello."

"Warren, Allen here. Matthews wants you and Shelly to come to the office at 11:00 for a meeting. Can you make it?"

"Yes, I'll be there."

"Thank you. I will see you then. He hung up."

Shelly and Warren started laughing. "Oh my God. I cannot believe he asked for you. I didn't know what to say." She had her hands over her face.

Still laughing, Warren said, "I guess that means we are busted."

"What do we do?"

"We go. It's a little after eight so we have time to eat and for you to go home to change."

"I brought a bag with me last night, Warren. I have a change of clothes."

"That's why I love you. We think alike. You shower first and I will cook up some breakfast."

"If you joined me," she said, "it would be faster." Shelly took his hand and pulled him to the bathroom.

"It definitely will not." He followed her in.

19
A Possibility

They were sitting in Davis's office. Matthews on one side, Day on the other. Davis was pacing behind his desk.

"Do you know why I called you both in?" Davis asked.

"Yes. we do." Warren tried to keep his composure the best he could. Shelly was having a harder time.

"What is your solution to this?"

Warren was not sure if it was a rhetorical question, so he remained silent.

"You two are outstanding agents, and I am in a spot right now. What am I supposed to do with you?"

Warren started to say something, then decided against it.

"Shelly, you have been an agent for years. Did you think it would go unnoticed?"

"No, sir, I did not."

"And yet—" Davis stopped.

Warren at this point had enough. "Sir, may I interrupt for a minute?"

Matthews looked over at Davis and nodded his head approvingly.

"What's on your mind, Warren?"

"As you know people are funny at times. You can never really know how they will react to each other. Especially partners. How many partners have you disliked through the years? I find it difficult to relate to people and to be comfortable with them. Shelly has been the only person that kept me focused. She is a very strong woman and is dedicated. I am an analyst that is now in the field trying to kill people. I feel safe with her around.

"Saying that, I am not a man who is gullible and naive enough to fall for the first woman that I meet. Our relationship may have started on adrenaline, but it has continued with much more. Let Shelly keep her job and do whatever you want with me. I am not trying to be noble; she is much more important to you than me. After a few more of these operations, other countries will be questioning whether the United States are somehow connected, and the program will end. I'm a computer guy. This is her life."

Davis was flustered. "All right, you two. Go home. I will talk to you later."

"Well?" Davis asked no one in particular.

Matthews shrugged. "He has a good argument."

"I don't know," Allen said. "Too much can go wrong. Chris, do you trust Shelly?"

"Yes, I do. You know her, Allen. She is a fine agent."

"Then what is she doing with Maypoole?"

"I can't answer that."

"I can," Henry threw out.

"Why is that, Henry?"

"Maypoole is an interesting man. He is awkward, I admit that, and he is a loner, but he is not a lonely man or troubled. He has friends and has dated his share of women, so he is not a frightened recluse. He is brilliant as you know. Look at the two assignments he was given. He stayed on track with no hesitation at all. He is very clever even outside his environment. He was able to solve an almost impossible problem, meaning he is stronger than we gave him credit for and is very resourceful. He is also not afraid to get close to danger if he needs to. Shelly saw this long before we ever would. Apparently, they bring out the best in each other."

Allen asked if they should remain a team.

"Yes. Originally, I had my doubts, but now I believe it may be beneficial."

"Warren was right," Chris said. "Too many accidents may become a problem for us."

"Agreed. We need to choose carefully from now on."

Allen said, "If we are going through with this, I will call them tomorrow and tell them to take some time off and come in next week."

"Call them tonight, Allen." Henry was worried about Warren. "Before they do something, we will regret. Like resign."

Allen made the call after his meeting. Shelly could not believe it. She was expecting dismissal or transfer, not, *we want you to continue*. She called for Warren in the other room.

"Are you serious? Both of us?"

"Yes, and we have a week off to go out as a couple for once."

"That means they are planning something for us. We will be going somewhere."

"That's true, but we can stay together. Are you happy?"

"Very. Are you?"

She put her arms around his neck and kissed him. "Yes, I am."

Taking advantage of their newfound freedom and no longer under the restraints of government regulations, they went to dinner, then a movie. They held hands while walking the streets unafraid. A full day was spent at the Smithsonian Institute, moving from building to building. It was exhausting, but they loved being able to share their interests.

They spent the night over at Shelly's house. This was the first time for Warren to see her house, and he was impressed. Just slightly smaller than Warren's, it was not as cluttered as his. He imagined she spent more time away then at home. Still it was comfortable. The cabinets and refrigerator were not stocked, proving his point.

Lying on the couch, they spoke of their families, schooling and growing up in different parts of the country. Warren was quiet for some time, and Shelly asked. "What's wrong?"

"I'm okay."

"Don't do that. What is it?"

"I was thinking of our assignments. Miami and Washington."

"Now? Why now? Should I be concerned?"

"Everyone is convinced that I have succeeded in creating the perfect and most clever accidents." Warren ran his fingers through her hair. It gave him time to gather his thoughts.

"I know Warren. I was there and saw what you were able to do."

"You saw what you wanted to see. I had no idea that mule was going to come onto the dam. I knew the dam had to come down, but at the time I didn't have an answer. So, it was an accident that an accident occurred."

Shelly thought for a moment. "So, you were going to destroy the dam to begin with."

"Yes, I was. Somehow."

"There was not a time limit, Warren. We were there for only three days."

"Maybe. This spy stuff is way over my head."

Shelly asked about Miami.

"Miami? That was unexpected."

"You had it all planned out. Even the times were perfect." She wondered why bring this up now.

Warren was embarrassed that he was confessing to his failures. However, he was not brave enough to bring up the fact the wrong man was targeted.

Shelly sat up, raised her voice, and said he was wrong.

"What you did was amazing, Warren. You knew your plan was complicated and relying on others is sometimes hard to predict how they'll react. Maybe it didn't work as planned, but it did work. What you do is design a plan, lay it out to make it clear, and by some chance it doesn't work, you're resourceful enough to do plan B. Even if you didn't have a B. That's how you think, Warren. You see it as a game with pieces and you assemble them. For example, if you were not on the dam, the mule would not have come over. When you left, did you think what would happen if someone else climbed on the dam?

"A little," Warren answered.

"Christ. Read your notes They are so detailed and exact. The data was there for you to set it all in motion. Be happy with that. Believe me, everyone tries to rethink the previous assignment."

80

Although Shelly was convinced what she was saying was true, Warren was not quite sure. In both instances, he was unaware what was taking place. Maybe she was right. Maybe he reacted fast enough to actually make it work. Be happy with that.

20

Keeping Busy

The next three days were lazy, quiet, and uneventful. Warren never brought up the accidents again. Shelly enjoyed herself being home. Their relationship grew stronger living as a family. Tomorrow was Monday, and they had a meeting in the morning with Allen.

When the meeting ended with Allen, Warren and Shelly were on their way to England. The target was a Syrian living there. They spent their time studying and collecting information. Seven days later the unfortunate Syrian met his demise in a terrible accident that even the English were baffled by.

Another assignment was in the West Indies. A small Island south of St. Thomas. Shelly was instrumental in pulling that one off. This was the first time she had complete control over an operation. Warren was sick and could not leave the hotel, so Shelly did all the leg work. She followed the man for three days, knew all his habits when, somehow, he was hit by a boat scuba diving.

No investigation was necessary. She was very proud with what she accomplished and so was Warren, even though a man had died.

After the two assignments they were allowed two weeks off at home until a new assignment was offered.

Matthews and Davis were never out of touch. Allen Day always wanted updates, constantly calling, not knowing there is a time difference in other countries.

It was never mentioned by Davis or anyone about their relationship. It seemed to quietly disappear, which suited Warren. He did not want to deal with the subject again.

They moved back into Warren's house for the remainder of their time off. For one reason his kitchen was well stocked. He liked to cook, therefore it was better to have a full refrigerator and cupboards for the right ingredients. Shelly definitely didn't mind Warren cooking. He was much better and patient.

One night while in bed she asked, "How are you holding up?"

"Fine, why? Don't you think I am?"

"You seem to be doing all right, Because, we leave soon."

"I'm fine, Shelly. Honest."

Shelly smiled at him. "I worry sometimes about you, that's all."

"Thank you." He held her tight. She was too quiet. He realized she was crying. "What is it, Shelly?"

She was wiping her eyes. "'m afraid that one day I will lose you. This is a dangerous game out there, and you are too casual about it. I'm sorry. I don't mean to be a baby. I am just being silly. I love you." For the first time she admitted how she felt. Warren was always telling her how much he loved her. He was comfortable saying it. She has never been. She was too frightened of the prospect of losing him in some foreign country or crazy accident.

"I love you too. I'll be all right."

She fell asleep in his arms. Happy for once.

21

Germany

Allen Day was waiting in his office for Warren and Shelly to show. He thought they should be well rested after a two-week break. He, Matthews, and Davis had been trying to decide on the next assignment. There was a lot to consider regarding which person should be targeted. They preferred someone to be traveling instead at their home. This person also had to be at the top on the list of priority. More important, though, to be in an area, Warren could work comfortably and safely. With very little restrictions.

They finally found what they had been searching for. A German with ties to almost every criminal activity in Europe. The German government contacted Matthews and asked if he could recommend someone to help out with a small problem. Two days later after a discussion with Allen and Henry, Matthews returned the call and asked if they would consider sending intel on the target. They agreed but would not want to be connected in anyway if something were to happen to this man. Matthews assured them they would not.

When Warren and Shelly arrived, Allen had all the necessary papers in hand and had made the travel arrangements. Their flight left at noon which gave them little time to prepare. Thankfully, Allen had a driver waiting. There was no need to go home to pick up baggage; they were getting used to the short notice. They made good time to the airport, stopped to get coffee and went through TSA. Boarding was time-consuming. It seemed everyone wanted to travel to Germany or Switzerland. Warren didn't know why they would. It was snowing and cold. Unless you skied, there was not much else to do in the winter.

They landed in Frankfurt, and hopped on a train north, then had to take a cab to a small town in the middle of nowhere. To Warren the name was unpronounceable. Close to the Alps, the town was snuggled in between large mountain ranges. The snow was already deep, and more was predicted. Shelly was in heaven. She stood in the center of the road and circled.

"It's beautiful here. Don't you think, Warren?"

"Yes, it is, but really cold."

"Come on, let's have some fun while we're here."

"Later. We have to check in before it gets too late."

Shelly frowned. "It's only 8:00 p.m. and the night is young."

"You're crazy. Come on, before you freeze."

"Old man," she said.

Inside they were greeted by an older woman who spoke very broken English. Warren tried to explain why they were there, but he didn't know if she understood. It was more like a bed and breakfast than a hotel. He assumed he would know why it was chosen in time. They went up to their room and realized it was cold and wondered where the furnace was.

A knock on the door furnished the answer. Warren answered and a man was shown in carrying a load of wood. He made three trips. piled it all in a corner and started a fire in the stove. Shelly was fascinated by all of this. She thanked the man and sat by the stove, waiting for the heat to thaw her. She was still so excited to be here. She was beaming with delight. Warren tried to settle her down, but she did not want to hear about it. The room was warming fast and Warren sat on the bed studying the file Allen had given them before they left.

Shelly picked up the file and read out loud for Warren to hear.

Carl Van Dyne. Born in Germany, Berlin to be exact, in nineteen sixty. Educated in Berlin for an engineering degree. Relocated to London and worked there for ten years before resigning and returning to Berlin. For reasons unknown, he dropped out of engineering, bought a few night clubs and a few other businesses in and around Berlin.

"Why is this Van Dyne so important?" Warren asked. "It seems he is just your average gangster, like in all the other cities around the world." Shelly handed him a sheet of paper to read. He skimmed through it. "Okay, I've got it. Apparently, Van Dyne deals in stolen goods, as in diamonds and paintings. Probably a lot more. But, still—"

"Warren. It says here that the German government will be supplying the intel for this operation. What do you think of that?"

"Wow. They approved this."

"As long as there are no repercussions to their government."

"Understandable, but how did they even know about us? Why did they know?"

Shelly tried to explain it. Davis or Matthews would never admit they helped. They probably told them they would look into it and if they heard of someone, they would pass the information along.

"I bet they know more than they are telling us, Shelly." Warren was walking around the room and stopped by the window to look out. "We have another problem."

"What's that?"

"Ice. It's sleeting hard out there. This will complicate things a little."

"It's late. Let's get some sleep and worry about this in the morning."

Warren woke not long after the fire went out. Jumping out of bed he reloaded the stove and started another fire. When he was satisfied it would stay lit, he was back under the covers. He looked at Shelly. She never moved. The alarm sounded at 7:00. Shelly made coffee and Warren threw more logs on the fire. They did not much care for the coffee. It was bitter and too strong for their taste but was hot. A knock on the door brought Warren away from the stove.

"Mr. and Mrs. Crawley," he heard from the other side of the door.

Warren opened the door, and the German woman held two trays for breakfast. It turned out her name was Marla. She set the trays on the table and left. Shelly was sitting and waiting. Warren burst out laughing.

"What's so funny?" she asked.

"I don't believe I've ever seen anyone eat like you. Especially a woman."

"I can't help it. I am always hungry."

Warren let her eat; he checked the fire then pulled back the curtains to the window.

"Shelly!"

Shelly walked to the window. "Oh my God! What do we do?"

Ice covered everything outside. Solid ice.

Warren pointed. "Look at that, on the rails. Must be three inches of ice. I can imagine what the roads are like."

A plow would have trouble cutting through.

"What do you think we should do?"

"Not much. All that ice on snow. It looks like we will be stranded for a while."

The hotel where they were staying was situated midway along a row of businesses and houses. A small street ran between a similar row across from it. At the corner sat a large circular open space, one hundred feet in diameter. The open space was empty with the exception of a large wooden wagon and an iron cart. Warren supposed the area was more like a center square for markets and gatherings. On the opposite corner from where Warren was standing stood a century-old structure. The hotel was painted on one of the walls facing the street. At the entrance, the porch roof extended fifteen feet. It was made of concrete and was supported by two wooden posts at the end. The roof obviously was very heavy. Probably added years after the building's construction.

Carl Van Dyne was the honored guest. Home away from home. Warren was sure Van Dyne had invested heavily in the restoration in the old building for his comfort. The intelligence they received from the Germans gave no indication where Van Dyne's rooms were located or the layout of the hotel. With the snow and ice, it would be impossible to establish what his routines were, or if he had one.

Warren showered and went down to the lobby while Shelly drank her coffee and surveyed the town from their window. It was a small room with a few couches and chairs, a table centered with smaller chairs to be used for cards. Books lined one wall, half in German the others a mixture of English, French, and lesser known languages. A fireplace sat in the corner that kept the room cozy. He sat on one of the sofas. Marla brought in a cup of coffee and some cakes. She asked how he was doing and apologized for the weather. They had a difficult but nice conversation on the weather and lack of activities because of it.

Warren said it was fine, he and Shelly would make the most of it. They would go out later to look around. Marla was adamant about not going out.

"Too cold today," she said. "Tomorrow."

Warren nodded yes. "Okay."

He sat on the sofa considering his options, knowing they were limited. After a while, he left to go back to his room.

Shelly was showered and dressed, sitting by the stove and reading a brochure for the area. He pulled a chair to the window so he would have a good view of that part of town. The sun was shining and reflected off the ice, making it hard to see in certain directions, he had to constantly adjust the chair. Both became increasingly pessimistic in thinking they could produce anything remotely resembling an outcome that would satisfy Davis and Matthews.

He turned to Shelly. "Anything interesting in that book?"

"Yes, but not for today. I am not shopping or hiking."

"I guess not. Why don't you call Allen to see what he wants us to do?"

"Why am I always calling Allen?"

"He likes you better."

"I don't know about that. I think he tolerates us, that's all," she said, all the while picking the phone up and making the call. She gave Allen the details on the situation, including the weather and lack of information to get them through this. "We need a little help, Allen."

"All right, sit tight, I will get back to you."

Shelly shrugged, put the phone down, and said, "I guess we wait."

They were eating their lunch when there was a knock on the door. They were expecting Marla but a man in a suit, carrying a briefcase stood at the doorway.

"Can I help you?" Warren asked the man.

The man looked around the room. He spotted Shelly. Good, I have the right room.

"Mr. and Mrs. Crawley?"

"Yes. Who are you?"

"My name is Joseph Faust. May I come in."

Shelly stayed far enough away, not sure what this man wanted. She watched as he walked to the table.

"My I sit, please?"

"Mr. Faust. What do you want?" Shelly sounded defensive.

"I'm sorry. Perhaps I should explain."

Warren stood behind him. "That would be a good place to start."

"My superiors received a call from an Allen Day requesting assistance, regarding a Mr. Van Dyne."

"In this weather?"

"I was very close by, so this is much better than a phone call."

"I thought there was someone around."

"How did you know?"

"Don't mind him, Mr. Faust. He's just showing off."

Faust looked a little confused. Shelly said, "Have a seat."

The three sat at the small table.

"What did you say to Marla downstairs?"

"I know most people in this town and for miles around. My wife and I own a small business here, so we see a lot of them. My real purpose is to keep tabs on Van Dyne."

"You just keep an eye on him?" Shelly didn't understand. "Why watch him and not do anything?"

"My government wanted to know who visits and where they go. My job basically was to monitor his vacation home and communicate anything unusual or potentially dangerous."

"So, why now?" Warren asked

"There has been a lot more activity in and around Berlin. The higher ups, as you Americans say, are getting nervous."

"How often does Van Dyne show up here?"

"At least once a month." Faust paused. "You, Mr. Crawley, do not look government."

"I am government. Not your average type. All I do is analyze information. She's the real one."

Shelly gave Warren a look. "Real one?"

"Yes. You're a real agent who works in the field. I just hang around."

Faust was completely confused now. "I have read both your files."

"And?" Shelly asked.

"We agreed to help because of your success on other assignments. We never would have suspected any foul play if we had not been told."

Warren wanted to know why their files were sent to them. "This was supposed to be confidential," he said.

"I don't know, Mr. Crawley, unless your government wanted to prove to us you were capable."

"I do not like to have my name all over the internet."

"Please, I assure you, it is not. We were very careful with your information."

Shelly raised her eyebrows, looking at Faust. "Do you have any intelligence that may help here?"

"Not a lot. I have never been able to see inside the hotel, but friends of mine have, so I can give you a good idea. Here is a file on Van Dyne." He handed Shelly the folder. "As you can see, he is involved in everything illegal. A bad man."

"Why can't your people take him out? Seems like it would be easy."

"Oh, it would be. At any time. He has friends and money. If he was killed, people would pay dearly. Physically, I mean. It would have to be a perfect accident. Otherwise, even people in government would ask questions. This day and age society does not appreciate that hard decisions sometimes need to be made for security and the safety of others. Anyway, Please, call me Joseph."

"Shelly and Warren."

"Really?"

"Really."

22

A New Friend

"**W**arren, Can I ask a favor of you, and perhaps of you too Shelly."
"What is it?"

"For my personal curiosity. Explain to me Bernelli."

"Shelly, would you like to take this one?" Warren was watching Joseph.

"Have you seen the tape, Joseph?"

"That's what intrigued me, I saw nothing that suggested it was not an accident."

"That is what accidents are, Joseph," Shelly commented.

"Indeed, Shelly, it is. I was told Warren spotted you early on at the hotel."

"He did. He is very clever when he wants to be."

"Yet, he said nothing?"

"No, he was playing with me, a game."

"Playing in what way?"

"He wanted me around. He left files on a table for me, so I could find them. I didn't have any luck the day before. He made sure I could see him make certain moves and to throw me off track at times."

"Were you aware he was doing all of this?"

"A little. I was not sure if he knew it was me or someone in the hotel. He is shy. I think he wanted a date. What did you call it Warren? Foreplay."

Joseph burst out laughing.

"Aside from that, though, Warren plays logic games, so he figured that since I was there, I may as well get involved."

Warren was enjoying the conversation.

"I am a bit confused on how the statue was used. I am sorry, Warren. You don't mind me addressing your wife, do you?"

"Not at all. She was there."

"Thank you."

"The way it was explained to me and the way I witnessed it was people react according to their attitudes and personalities. Their behavior is predictable. The hotel in Miami was very high class and the guests were spoiled and arrogant. Warren used the guests as part of the plan, and their involvement was necessary for the plan to work. The statue was the key to the plan, and with only one support, how could it be knocked out in order for the statue to fall. Remember the woman at the pool?"

"Yes, the one your husband was holding."

"Don't smile, Warren;" Then Shelly did. "He held on to her long enough for the cart to come by. The fat man would never push a guest, but he would an employee. She was beneath him. Warren had to rely on people being themselves to make it work."

Faust was shocked. "You could not have anticipated or expected it to work. What if the woman did not come out of the pool? What if the fat man did not walk by? Warren turned to answer Joseph."

"Joseph, you're right. I could not guarantee it would work. Too many variables. However, I had one chance, and that was it. Bernelli was in the tent for an hour, I knew who was in the pool, along the pool, I knew where the cart was, and the distance from the statue. The woman did not complain being held that long, and the noise from when the fat man hit the cart and everyone screaming, all the attention was on him. Everyone saw from that moment."

"What if you calculated wrong?"

Warren thought for a minute. "I would have hit the cart somehow. Same result."

"So, you deal with chances?"

"Not necessarily. With the data I collect and observations I can design a series of actions to take place. Then I add the pieces as I go along. Joseph, I am an analyst and I do games. I am not an agent. I have to think logically no matter what."

"That's extraordinary. Law of averages."

"And a chain of events, Joseph. All I can do is put something in motion and see what happens. If not, I push a little."

Joseph tried to put the pieces together. He was not sure how much of the explanation he could believe. Having read the file, though, he had to acknowledge the results.

"Thank you, both of you. I didn't mean to take up your time with this. It is a wonderful story."

Joseph was looking at his file, deciding what to say. "Getting back to Van Dyne, because of the weather, I doubt if he will stick to his regular schedule."

"What is at the rear of the hotel? Is there anything that would help?" Warren wanted to know how it laid out.

"There is a porch with tables and one door. The woods start maybe fifty yards back.

Shelly asked, "How many bodyguards?" She thought as an agent and was always thinking of safety.

"I guess it depends on their plans, it varies. Also, what guests show up for the week. There are two guards now with him. This is a bad location, especially with the weather. Sorry."

Shelly thought they were going in this blind.

"Joseph, Warren has been looking out the window all morning and he does not seem too confident. Maybe we ought to concede this for now."

"I agree. This could be a bad omen."

Warren was pacing the room. Alone in his thoughts.

"Warren!" Shelly yelled.

"What?"

"Are you listening to what we are talking about?"

"Yes, I am."

"Then what do you think?"

Shelly's phone rang. "Hold on. I'll get it."

Warren held the phone to his ear. "Hello."

Shelly watched as his mood changed.

"No! He can't now." Warren dropped the phone and ran into the bedroom. Shelly and Joseph jumped to their feet.

"Warren, what's wrong?"

"He's leaving."

"Who is leaving?"

"Van Dyne. That was Allen on the phone. They intercepted a call from someone, and they said Van Dyne was ready to leave the hotel."

"It's not going to be that easy for him. I'll be back."

When he came out of the bedroom, he was wearing his coat and boots. Grabbing his hat and gloves he kissed Shelly and ran out the door.

Shelly and Joseph remained standing and stared at the closed door.

"What do we do, Shelly?"

She cleaned the table and opened a bottle of water and sat again.

"We wait."

Joseph put more wood on the fire and sat with her.

"Do you think we should help him?"

"Nothing to do right now. We would be in the way and a distraction."

"What if he needs help? He is not trained."

"He needs me before and after, not during. I usually don't know what he is thinking or has planned. Sometimes I don't think he does. He does have a bad habit of getting too close, though. So, I do have to watch him. He always comes back to me. We can watch from here."

They stood at the window looking towards Van Dyne's hotel. "Warren will show up soon. She knew he saw something staring at the hotel all that time. She was sure.

"The two of you complement each other. Each have your own abilities and way about you. I find you an interesting couple." Joseph was being very sincere.

"I think we work well together."

"From what I heard, even more."

Jesus, are they telling everyone?"

Joseph laughed.

Warren appeared below them, walking slowly because of the ice. He was passing an old wagon. A large one with wooden spoked wheels. Similar to a Conestoga without the canvas top. He looked around, then approached it. He circled a few times, and they saw him kick at the wheels. Warren found a wooden post and tried using it as a lever to slide it forward. The wagon was frozen in the ground. He then tried it on all four sides. It didn't look like it budged at all.

As Warren turned to move away, his feet went out from beneath him. He landed on his back.

Shelly said, "Ouch. That's going to hurt."

Fifty feet to the other side was another cart. This was a steel one that connected to the rear of a truck. It was loaded with bricks and ice. Warren tried to move it by kicking it on all sides. He leaned at the back and tried to push.

"What is he trying to do?" Joseph asked.

"I am really not sure."

They saw Warren turn quickly towards the hotel. They could see the door to the hotel start to open and two men exited.

Warren tried to move a little too fast but ended up on the ground. He landed hard and was sliding feet-first fast down the hill in the direction of the hotel. He spun around and slammed into the wall by the entrance of the hotel just missing the two men. The men jumped back, and one pulled out a handgun.

Shelly grabbed Josephs arm. "No, what is he doing?"

Joseph answered, "What you have been saying to me. Setting it in motion."

"You're right." Shelly relaxed a little. The man put his gun away. Two women ran out the door to check on Warren. He had a cut over his eye and one of the women had a tissue to stop the bleeding. Shelly saw the woman turn and speak to the men and they helped Warren to his feet.

Farther down the road, a Mercedes was making its way up the hill. They could see the chains on the tires, it was having no problem on the ice. It was obvious, the car was for Van Dyne.

A few more people came out and stood under the awning. One man was clearly Van Dyne. From their window they could see Van Dyne and Warren in a conversation.

Shelly grabbed two pairs of field glasses from her bag, for Joseph and herself. She did not want to miss anything.

If Warren needed her help, she would be there for him.

There were now six people, not including Warren under the awning. Suddenly, a woman screamed, a high-pitched sound that made everyone jump. At first no one knew why she was screaming, then they heard the cart rolling down on them. The ice crackling under its wheels.

Everyone under the awning backed to the door and saw the cart crash into the post at the end.

It hit the post so hard it came off the foundation and fell to the ground. They could see the relief on the faces when the awning held. It was quite a scene seeing the cart continue on down the hill. The Mercedes stopped then tried to turn as the cart was rolling in its path. It was not quick enough. The cart caught the driver's front light and bumper and ricocheted down the hill.

Joseph said, "Damn. It missed."

"Not necessarily, Joseph, it's never like it seems. It is always the second one."

The stunned crowd was staring in the direction of the car. The driver was standing outside waving his hands and shouting. Van Dyne motioned for him to come. The car moved forward then stopped. Van Dyne motioned again.

All the attention was focused on the car and driver, no one noticed the wagon that was speeding down right at the crowd. Warren saw it. The women screamed again the instant the wagon was on them. He grabbed the women and pushed them as far back to the door as he could as the wagon hit the remaining support and carried it away. The awning collapsed instantly creating chaos everywhere.

The front entrance was blocked by the rubble the ones inside had to find another exit. The street was filling fast with people wanting to help. Shelly and Joseph had their coats on and running to the door, and when they made it to the street, they realized how slippery the ice was. There was a crowd of people trying to remove the debris in hopes there would be someone still alive. They saw Warren with the two women on the ground, he was holding them close. The women were hysterical. They could see blood on their clothes and there was no sign of the men.

Joseph took hold of Warren's arms and carried him far enough away from the damaged awning and sat him down. Shelly helped the women along with other residents and they walked them to safety.

The ambulances arrived soon afterward, and they rolled Warren on a cart into one of them. Shelly climbed in the back as they rode off to the hospital. The women were also taken. Joseph said he would meet them there.

23

The Debriefings Brief

At the hospital they received news that four men had died. Including Van Dyne. The women had suffered no serious injuries and were to be released soon. Warren had a gash on his cheek and a few minor cuts. His left arm would be in a sling for a while, aside from that he was in good shape. The news that Warren had saved the two women was out and many people came to the hospital with flowers to thank him.

Warren was released from the hospital, and Joseph dropped them at the door of their hotel. Joseph said he was glad Warren was all right and he would see them later after he went home to make a few calls. Shelly told him to bring his wife over to have dinner. In the hotel, Marla hugged and kissed him for helping the women. She said it was a shame the men did not make it. Marla told them she would bring a good dinner up to them and some wine.

"Can you bring enough for Joseph and his wife? They will be here soon."

"Oh yes. I like Joseph and Luca."

Warren looked at Shelly. "Luca?"

"I guess that's her name."

The room was almost hot from the stove, but after today they welcomed it. Marla must have been here getting ready for their return.

Warren sat on the sofa. Shelly sat next to him and said, "If you ever do something that stupid again, I'll be the one to kill you."

"It wasn't that bad. I am sorry the others had to die. I didn't expect it." She kissed him long and told him she was frightened to death when the awning came down.

"You cannot die yet. We aren't even married yet."

"Do you want to get married?"

Shelly stammered. "What?"

"Marry me. As soon as things settle."

"You are crazy. Did they give you drugs there?"

"Hey, you mentioned it first. I love you. You love me. Let's do it soon."

She wrapped her arms around him. "Of course, I will marry you, but not until you are healthy."

"Deal."

"Wait, what about Matthews."

"We can find work anywhere. Right."

There was a knock on the door. "Hold that thought, mister."

Marla entered with trays of food.

"Good German food for health." She placed them on the table.

Five minutes later she brought four bottles of wine.

"Thank you, Marla. That's sweet." Shelly walked her to the door. As Marla was leaving, Joseph and his wife came in.

"Come on in, Joseph."

"Shelly, this is my wife, Luca. That's Warren. The injured one."

Warren walked over and shook both their hands. "Hi, Luca. Pleasure to meet you."

"Thank you, Warren."

Luca was as tall as Shelly, very attractive and spoke perfect English. At one time she and Joseph worked for the government but resigned to marry and help run their business. "What is your business, Luca?" Shelly asked.

"We have a small jewelry store here in town. Enough to pay the bills, plus Joseph still receives pay from the government. I think you cost Joseph his job, Warren."

"Sorry. Ironic, isn't it?"

The four sat at the table as Shelly passed around plates and silverware. Luca poured the wine and asked how Warren was.

"I am fine. Sore, but it could be worse."

"Warren," Joseph said. "You are one crazy man. You know that."

"Why is that?"

"One minute we were sitting here saying we should abort the whole operation, then you go running outside on the ice with no plan, and no hope to the hotel."

They all laughed except Warren.

"I had a plan. Granted it wasn't much of one, but I gave a shot."

"I have no idea what to send to Berlin. They will be expecting a report tomorrow."

"I always have that problem with him, Joseph." Shelly punched Warren's arm. "Even after he explains it, I can't really put it in a report that makes sense."

Warren looked at Joseph. "Did you watch it all?"

"Yes, of course, but I cannot see how you managed it."

Luca was excited. "Please, Warren, tell us how you arranged it."

Warren took a deep breath. "Do you want the official or unofficial?"

Shelly was listening but ate her dinner. With her mouth full she said, "Go on. I want to hear it too. Official first, please."

"All right. You know we did not have time or information, no offense." Joseph nodded. "I had been sitting at the window most of the morning. The inside of the hotel was not going to help, so I decided the only course of action was that it needed to be done on the outside. I needed time, though, to think it through. After Allen called, time was something I no longer had. The cart and the wagon were there. The awning at the entrance was there. That was the extent of my plan."

"That wasn't much of one," Shelly joked.

"I knew the awning had to be the key if I could accomplish anything. It was made of concrete and was supported by the two posts. From what I could tell they were sitting on the foundation, not in the ground. so, I thought knocking one off would be enough. I was wrong. The wagon was frozen solid, but I was at least able to shift it.

"The cart was easier, but the bodyguards came at an inopportune time. If they saw me by the cart the plan was over, so I got to the ground and slid to the hotel. It was a little too fast, and I hit the wall next to them, but I was lucky the women came, or the men might have shot me. I exaggerated the slide and my injury for the benefit of the women and guards because I needed time and counted on the cart hitting first. It might have missed completely, I wasn't sure. When it did slide and hit the post, I expected it to come down. What helped, the Mercedes driving to the hotel and the cart smashing into it, and it was the perfect distraction. I intended for it to make the driver nervous, but it worked out better."

"I also needed to keep all the guests occupied, so I was telling them all to look at the cart as it bounced off the car and down the road. I was the only one paying attention to the wagon and when the woman turned and screamed, it was already too late."

Joseph stopped him. "So, you planned on the wagon hitting the first post?"

"No."

"You just said—"

"I had no idea."

"What were you waiting on?"

"I wasn't sure."

"How does that work, Warren?" Luca chimed in.

"Listen. The official version is what I told you. It was all planned and with a little luck it worked. No one will argue with you. A chain of events is exactly what it is. Unofficially, I had no idea what I was doing."

The three of them laughed hard. They realized Warren was serious. Disbelief was not the word. They were stunned.

Luca asked, "You accomplished what you set out to do, how can you say that?"

"How much time did I have?"

"None."

"I did know the awning was heavy, and that the posts were vulnerable. I knew Van Dyne would be standing there waiting for his car, and I would be there. With all of that in mind, and what I calculated, something had to happen. I set in motion everything I thought of, in the amount of time I had. And of course, I was there to help it along if needed. A friend from Miami once said 'What are the chances?' I agree. It was a wild guess, I admit that, almost pure luck. Just don't spread it around."

Luca was still trying to grasp what he said. "Shelly is this how it works all the time."

Not all the time, but sometimes, no matter how he explains, I still can't understand. Even with me watching from the beginning it looks like it was set up, but I always ask, how could it? We usually have a week to prepare for something like this. This assignment was not normal or fun."

"I don't know, Warren." Luca was still confused. "It was more than luck."

"I don't know, Luca. Yes and no. If I hadn't been working on the wagon and the cart, nothing would have happened. So, was it luck? If I had not been under the awning, would it have happened? I doubt it. The fact that it actually worked, maybe that was luck. Who knows? Accidental accidents."

Joseph smiled at Shelly and repeated, "Accidental accidents. The perfect description, Warren."

For the next few hours, they drank wine and told stories. They agreed to spend time over the Fausts' house the next day.

It turned out, Joseph and Luca were good friends. They shared a wonderful dinner together and spent the rest of the evening enjoying their company. A promise was made to see each other as soon as they found time.

24

Back Home Again

Once again, by the time they arrived in Washington, they were exhausted. Warren told Allen they needed a day to sleep. It was two.

The official debriefing was always separate. Shelly told her side and Warren his, but with a bit more detail. Both Washington and the Germans were pleased with the outcome, though the Germans wanted more of an explanation on how it was done. Matthews told them Warren had his ways and somethings were confusing. As long as he had results, they were not too concerned.

Matthews was not happy to hear Warren charged down onto the ice thinking something had to be done. He should have had Shelly with him.

"There was no time at all for me to explain, and I only had a few minutes to plan," Warren said, trying to defend himself. "My plan did not come together until I was out seeing if the wagon could be moved."

"Never again, Warren. Understand? That is an order."

Warren was on the sofa taking a nap and Shelly was reading. They were told they had two more days to rest and then off to somewhere else.

When it looked as though Warren was waking up, Shelly lay beside him.

"You know, Warren, I was so frightened when that wagon hit the awning."

"I know. I'm sorry. I saw it coming and figured I had time, but you would not have known it from where you were standing."

"That's not the point."

"I know it wasn't rational. It just seemed like something had to be done. Quickly."

"Even Matthews said no more charging the enemy."

Warren changed the subject. "When do you want to get married?"

It had not been mentioned since Germany, and with the flight home and the debriefing, they really haven't had time to discuss it.

"I'm not sure. Of course, I want to get married, but there is a lot to consider. Work, being at the top of the list."

"Policy forbids us to marry. I understand why, so I cannot complain."

"Warren, I can resign. You can still work as an analyst, and I could find work outside."

"No way. You can't resign. This is what you trained for. It's part of your life, so if anyone resigns it would be me."

"We fell in love by accident and for six months now we have been leading up to this point. The answer will come to us when we need it to. Let's get married in the early summer, that will give us five months to plan."

Warren kissed her. "There're never any problems, just minor inconveniences."

"Who said that?"

"I did. You like it?"

"I like you."

"Same thing. I like you too."

25
Change of Direction

Matthews received a call from Davis that morning who seemed unusually anxious and wanted to see him in his office as soon as possible. Allen was also told to come by.

They met in Davis's office twenty minutes later. Davis was not at his desk as usual. He paced behind his chair, then leaned against the wall looking at a file in his hand.

"Jesus, Henry. What's got into you?" Chris asked as he walked in the room.

"Have a seat, Chris. Allen will be here in a minute."

They didn't have long to wait. Allen came in and sat.

"I received a call from our friends in Britain and France wanting information about Van Dyne's death. France was hinting that maybe Bolon's accident was curious also."

Chris asked if this was just France fishing.

"I believe it was. I denied it of course. They couldn't possibly link the two. Even so, they are relieved they're gone."

Allen interrupted. "Henry, I have been thinking that maybe there have been too many accidents. I know the investigators have all ruled them having no signs of foul play. They are all very clean. Warren and Shelly were fantastic pulling these off...."

"But?"

"The odds of five international gun runners and smugglers all dying in six months are impossible."

"So, what are you suggesting, Allen?"

"As I said, Warren and Shelly have done amazing work, far beyond our expectations, but in my opinion too many, in such a short period of time. You received two calls so far. If this continues, more will follow."

Chris didn't like where this was going. "So, we just stop?"

"Unless you want to advertise around the world what we do."

"Any options?"

"Why don't we postpone things for a while." Henry did not want to draw suspicion from more countries. Including his own.

Allen added. "You know there are a lot of people that will be looking over their shoulders from now on. Maybe this is a benefit."

"Perhaps," Henry said. "Chris, do you want to call Shelly? I'll call Warren."

The calls were made, Warren and Shelly were thrilled at the decision to stop the operations.

26

An Unexpected Event

Shelly was grocery shopping, and Warren decided to catch up on some reading, something he had not been able to do for some time. A knock on the door brought him to his feet, and he opened the door. Three men pushed their way in, then closed the door. One man had a gun and pointed it towards Warren.

"Are you Fredrick Crawley?"

Warren was frightened and not sure how to answer.

"My name is Warren."

The man with the gun motioned to the others who started searching the house. they pulled books out, went through his desk and filing cabinets.

"Why are you looking for me? Why kill me?" Warren was definitely puzzled. His face must have shown it. "I don't even know who you are."

"My name is Francis Bezos."

"Sorry, it doesn't help."

"I was told Crawley was coming for me."

"Mr. Bezos, do I look like I am going anywhere? I am getting married in two days and am not going on my honeymoon looking for someone. Why would you even look here? My name is and always has been Warren Maypoole."

The two men came into the room and said they were satisfied. "His name is Maypoole. Here is his marriage license."

"Perhaps," Bezos said. "Maybe my information is inaccurate."

Warren knew he could not fight his way out of this. These men were bigger, stronger, and they had guns. Warren asked why he believed someone was trying to kill him.

"A friend of mine died a while ago. It was ruled an accident, but I am not sure. Crawley's name came up. Another man was also killed not long after. That too was ruled an accident."

"Crawley?"

"Yes, Crawley."

One of the men said, "Boss let's get out of here. It's clean."

"All right, let's go. Sorry, Mr. Maypoole. A person in my business cannot take chances."

He pointed the gun at Warren and pulled the trigger. The bullet entered just above the sternum. He fell back against the couch and fell to his side. The men were gone.

27
The Alarm

Shelly was at the front door; her hands were full of the groceries. She was kicking the door yelling for Warren to help.

"Warren, I need help." There was no answer. "Come on, Warren," she yelled. "My hands are full."

She put the bags on the ground and pulled her keys out of her purse. "Warren, are you home?" She saw Warren on the couch, lying on his side. "Are you all right?"

Then she saw the blood.

"No!" she screamed. "No."

She rolled him over, his shirt was soaked with blood. Checking his pulse, she was relieved. He was still alive.

Shelly picked up her phone and called 911.

"Man, thirty-six, gunshot wound to the chest." Her training helped, but this was her fiancé. She gave the address. "Make it quick, please."

Then she called Allen.

"Allen, Shelly. Warren's been shot."

"What do you mean, shot? Where are you? Is he alive? What about you?"

"I just got home and found him."

"I'll meet you at the hospital. I'll call Davis and Matthews."

Allen didn't waste any time. He called Davis first.

"How the hell did he get shot at home? How is he?"

"I don't know. Shelly is waiting for the ambulance."

"Is she all right?"

"She is fine. She found him."

"Christ. I'll meet you there. Call Chris for me."

Allen repeated the conversation with Matthews and his reaction was about the same.

He would stay at the office. If they find out anything let him know and he would get people on it.

The ambulance pulled close to the house, and they were able to get Warren on to the stretcher and on the road in minutes.

Shelly rode with him, holding his hand trying to stay calm for him. Warren opened his eyes.

"Oh, Warren, you will be all right. We'll be at the hospital soon."

He slid his oxygen mask to the side and whispered, "Bezos."

"What does that mean?"

"His name." Then he lost consciousness.

They got to the hospital and wheeled him into the operating room.

Shelly thought she would break down any minute. Allen came up behind her, put his arms around her shoulders. Shelly cried. "Allen, I can't believe this happened in our house."

"Did Warren say anything at all?"

"He mentioned a name. Bezos. Have you heard of him?"

Davis walked up. "Shelly, have you heard anything?"

"No, nothing," she said, sniffling. "He has been in the operating room for about twenty minutes."

"Where was he hit?"

"In the chest; close up by the looks of it."

"What do we know?"

"Just a name. Warren said the name Bezos."

"Let me call Chris. Have him ask around. He is waiting to hear from us."

While Davis was on the phone, the doctor came out. He walked over to Shelly.

"Doctor, how is he?"

"He lost a lot of blood. We got the bullet—9mm. Now we wait."

Davis came and showed the doctor his badge.

The doctor was surprised. "CIA, what are you doing here?"

"He is also," Davis said, nodding toward the operating room.

"I understand. We'll do everything we can. Right now, we have to wait. Miss," he said, looking at Shelly, "we will let you know when you can see him."

"Thank you, doctor."

Davis took Shelly's hand and walked her to a waiting room off to the side. Allen followed and they sat.

Davis told them what he and Chris discussed.

"Chris put his men on this man Bezos. They will find out all they can on him. At this time all we know is he is Italian, and they think he is a weapons smuggler. Why he came for Warren we have no idea. Chris also has a team working at Warrens house. Maybe we'll luck out."

Shelly was trying to control herself. This was too much.

"I was only gone a half an hour. They had to have been looking for something."

Allen was clearly upset. For six months they worked together. Although not the best of friends, he always liked the couple and was a little envious of their relationship and the fact they worked well as a team.

Allen said he would speak to the police to keep it quiet and ask for their help.

"Thank you, Allen, and thank you Henry."

Shelly tried to grasp what had happened.

"When we are in the field, there is always the possibility and you prepare for it. This was unexpected."

"What can I do, Henry?" Allen asked. Warren was his man and was shot. "This seems more like a hit than a random shooting."

"You're right," Henry said. "It does but no one should know about Warren and Shelly."

"Someone does."

"Allen, do whatever you need to and find out how his name was leaked. That's important. Call Germany. They were the only one to know his identity, besides us of course. If it came from our office, I want to know."

"My pleasure, Henry."

Henry stood to leave. He held Shelly's hand.

"I am going to see Chris at the office and try to manage this. If you hear anything, call me. Warren will be fine."

"Thanks, Henry."

Allen followed, "Bye, Shelly. I will be back later."

Henry asked Allen. "What do you think?"

"We were very careful. All the accidents worked perfect. I don't understand. Do you think there was a leak?"

"Hate to say it, but it had to be. If there was, find it, Allen."

"Yes, sir."

A nurse came out and led Shelly to Warren's room. He was alive and fighting, she thought. She sat by his side and held his hand. Two hours later when Allen returned, she had not moved.

"Any change?"

"None. Any leads?"

"A few. Apparently, Bezos worked with Bernelli. The thing is, though, Warren used his own name on that assignment, so was Bezos looking for Warren or Crawley?"

"That's true, Allen. I can't answer that. Only one person can." Shelly rubbed Warren's forehead and tears began to fall.

"Shelly, he's alive. Give him time. I will come back in the morning to see how he is. You should go home and get some rest."

"I can't right now." She half smiled.

"Okay. I'll see you then."

Warren was stable and was expected to recover from his wound, but it would take time before he could move around much. For three days she stayed at his bedside, leaving for a short time, to shower and make some calls. On the fourth day he opened his eyes.

"Oh, Warren, you're awake." He moved his eyes around scanning the room.

"Hospital?"

"Yes, hospital. Four days."

"I thought I was gone."

"You almost were, but you are back."

"Water please."

"Let me get the nurse."

She left and came back with a nurse in tow.

The nurse was all smiles. "Mr. Maypoole, you came back to us. The lovely lady hasn't left your side since you arrived." Then to Shelly, she said, "Maybe now you can get some sleep in a real bed at home instead of this old chair."

She let Warren have a little water and took his vitals. "Get some rest, Mr. Maypoole. That is what you need."

When the nurse left, Shelly called Allen. He said he would be over soon.

Warren was looking at her. "What do you want, Warren?"

"You."

"You already have me."

Warren whispered, "I am sorry to put you through this."

Shelly scowled at him. "It's not your fault; you know that. Stop with the crazy talk." Warren nodded.

Warren was still terribly weak, so Shelly did all the talking. It was good for her to talk to him. She was so happy.

Luca Faust called Shelly. She had just heard about Warren. They were both very sorry and saddened by the shooting and wanted to know if there was anything they could do.

"We will know more in a couple of days." She would have Warren call them when he is up to it.

Warren woke two hours later. Shelly was there along with Allen Day.

Allen was grinning. "Good to have you back. We were all worried. Too close, Warren."

Warren nodded yes.

"I am sorry, but you know what I have to do. All right?"

"Go ahead."

"Shelly?"

"He can talk a little."

"Can you tell me what happened?"

It was difficult to talk, but Warren did the best he could. He stopped occasionally to sip water. He could recall most of the conversation with Bezos and more came to him as he spoke.

"Anything implied or hinted at?"

"Not that I remember."

"He just shot you and left?"

"He said he couldn't take any chances."

"Did they find anything in your house?"

"No. The men said they were satisfied and wanted to leave. Bezos is the one who fired the gun."

"That's strange. Let me tell you what we found. Bezos worked with Bernelli and after his death he became worried that it would invite others to challenge him as head of the organization. There have been many deaths reported, and they believe Bezos is clearing any one out that does look to be ambitious enough to move in. The problem is, they had no intentions at all. I don't know if he is paranoid or delusional, but it is making the people in Italy very nervous. We believe he is in Florence staying in a large apartment complex, hiding out. We think your name was leaked from our office. That person will be found. That's the short version. Get some rest. I'll visit again. Shelly, walk me out. They walked to the waiting room. How do you think this will affect him?"

"I don't know. It's too soon. Anyone involved in a shooting is required to go to therapy. That won't be for a while. He will be in the hospital for a few more weeks."

"How are you holding up?"

"Better now." She smiled.

"I spoke to Henry and Chris. They are taking it hard. Warren was liked by everyone and they respected him. He is part of the family of agents. We don't like to lose anyone."

"I know, and Warren loved working there. We'll see if he wants to remain when this is over."

"Well, the program is over, obviously, we can't continue now that this has happened. He'll be back to his computer."

"Allen, do you think we will find out who leaked his name?"

I'll find him, or her. We have been silent on his condition and other details not to let on. By the way. We have an agent posted at his room until we are sure he's safe."

"Thanks. This is crazy. What should I do?"

"Go home and get some sleep. Eat a good dinner. Warren needs you healthy."

"You're right. I'll say goodbye to him and leave. Thank you."

"You're welcome. I will stop by tomorrow."

Shelly went to check on Warren; he was sound asleep. She kissed him and grabbed a taxi for home.

She showered, crawled into bed, and slept peacefully through the night.

28

Another Direction

A week after Warren regained consciousness, his appetite improved and was getting stronger. He and Shelly spent hours making plans to get married. Now it was moved to late summer. Shelly phoned her friends to set up shopping days. They were all excited that she was finally getting married and wanted to plan her days.

She needed a dress and shoes, a church and a venue for a reception after.

Shelly was so energetic, phone calls and lunches with friends. She called Luca to share the good news. They had to decide where to live once they were married; one house would have to be sold. Warren suggested they sell both and buy another.

The sad part was, Warren was being held captive in his room and probably would stay that way for a week or two. With Shelly gone, he called Allen and asked him to drop by.

Allen walked in. "Hey, what's up? You all right?"

"Yes, I'm fine. You have been a good friend the past couple weeks. I wanted to thank you."

"Not necessary, Warren."

"I have a favor to ask."

Allen looked at Warren. Curious. "Okay."

"I am not allowed to leave this place, but I need a few things at the store."

"That's no problem. What do you need?"

"You know we are making plans for the wedding."

"Shelly's running all over. She is so excited. That is all she is talking about, that and shopping."

"I know. That's why I need help."

"Go on."

"I need you to buy a ring for me to give to Shelly."

"Seriously. Can't you wait?"

"I'm sorry to ask, but she is working so hard for this now, but there's no engagement ring. I think that would make her happy."

"I'll get you one, Warren. You are one good man. Tell me what you want."

That evening Allen slid the ring under Warren's pillow and slipped out of the room.

Shelly came in and asked, "Was that Allen that just left?"

"Yes, he said he would see us tomorrow."

The ring was under the pillow too far; he couldn't reach it.

"What are you doing, Warren?" Shelly asked, laughing at him trying to move around.

Shelly ran her hand under the pillow searching for whatever it was.

"I found it. Something." She pulled out the ring case. "Oh my God, Warren." She pulled out the ring and put it on. "It's beautiful. I love you." She kissed him over and over. "Wait a minute. How did you get this?"

"Allen helped. Besides, we can't have a wedding without a ring."

"It's perfect. I'll have to thank him."

"Hey, I paid for it."

"I know, Warren. Now I have to go and show it off to all my friends."

"All this work that needs to be done and I cannot get out of here to help."

"Oh, honey. You are healing fast. A couple of weeks and you will be out. Give me a kiss and say goodbye."

One hundred channels later the television was turned off. Warren made a call from a burner phone a friend picked up for him.

"Faust here."

"Joseph, Warren."

"Good to hear from you. How are you feeling?"

"Much better, thanks."

"Shelly called Luca yesterday. They spoke for an hour about the wedding. I think it's great. You both deserve it."

"Thank you, Joseph. We are excited and looking forward to it. I need a small discreet favor."

"What's that?

"I need Bezos's address."

"You are kidding, right? What are you thinking?"

"I'm not sure," Warren replied.

"Shelly will kill you."

"Of that I am sure. I'll talk to her."

"Let me find out what I can. I'll get back to you. Take care."

"Thank you, my friend."

When Shelly finally returned from her day shopping, she looked tired.

"Hi, you look beat."

"I am. We went shopping, looking at dresses and everything we could think of. We looked at churches, but I think we have time before we decide on one."

"Wow. How many in the wedding party?"

"Only four girls now. I'm trying to keep it small, but I know it will grow."

"Wish I could help."

"Oh, you can. She handed him a pile of brochures. Help pick out a restaurant. A nice place for the reception. not too fancy, but nice."

Warren laughed. "For how many. A hundred?"

"About."

"A hundred. I was kidding. Do we know that many people?" He was shocked.

"You would be surprised, mister."

"I would. We'll see. Have you spoken to Allen?"

She leaned back on the chair and put her feet on the bed.

"Almost forgot. Matthews called. They found the one working with Bezos. A woman."

"He isn't sure why, but they will find out. Bezos was the only one who received the information, and they don't think he told anyone else. We lucked out."

"Do I know her? Do you?"

"Never heard of her. She works under Matthews so you can imagine he is not very happy."

"I suppose not," he said quietly. "Doesn't make much sense does it?"

"No, not at all. Allen will figure it out."

The nurse came in with a wheelchair. "Hi, Shelly. I have to steal your man for a while for tests. I'll bring him back safe."

"Have fun."

Shelly started straightening the room and the tables around the bed to keep occupied. She put all of his books in a pile by the bed, moved his empty tray. Under a box of uneaten chocolates, she found his burner phone. She opened it. There were no numbers called or received. He'd deleted all of them.

She sat on the chair and held on to the phone.

Warren came in smiling and in good spirits. "The doctor says I'm fine. I—What's wrong? You do not look happy."

Shelly leaned forward and handed him the phone.

Warren realized he should have told her earlier. She stuck by him through all this.

"Who have you been talking to? Joseph?"

"Yes," and that's as far as he got.

"When were you going to tell me?"

"When I heard something."

"Does Allen or Davis know?"

"Are you kidding? That's why the phone. They probably are monitoring my calls, so I don't do anything stupid."

"Why would they think that?" she threw at him sarcastically.

"I would have told you sooner, honest. I don't have anything at the moment. I just asked him to find Bezos."

"He is in Florence."

"I am aware of that. It's a pretty big city." Shelly thought for a moment. She jumped on the bed, and jolted Warren to a sitting position. "Ouch. What on earth are you doing?"

"You know, don't you?" Shelly said.

"What do I know?"

"You have a plan. I know you, Warren. You have had all day, every day to sit and think. Even without much information you can still do it."

Warren just sat there looking at her.

Shelly continued. "Yes, you can. Not the details or the how, but "what" you want to do to him."

"It's complicated."

"I bet. How many people do you need to help?"

"What! you want to help?"

"He tried to kill my husband, my fiancé. You cannot do this alone; you can hardly walk. I was afraid you would give up and not go after him. You never mentioned it. I have been waiting for you to go. If you didn't do it because of me, you would always be unhappy."

Warren pulled her to him and said, "I love you."

"I know. I am still angry, don't push me."

"Yes, ma'am. What about the wedding?"

"We never set a date. In the summer would be nice. Give me your phone. I'll call Luca."

"I will see you in the morning."

29

Last Plan

Shelly had her shower early the next morning, made some eggs and coffee and watched the news. The burner phone rang, and she answered it.

"Hello." No answer. "Joseph is that you?"

"Shelly, hi. How did you—"

"I found it. He had to confess to what he was planning."

"So, I guess you are in?"

"Yes, I am. What do you have?"

"I have a friend in Italy sent me Bezos address and a little more. They told me to stay away, not to get involved. He is not a rational man. Very unstable and unpredictable. Especially now."

"Why now, Joseph?"

"They say he is locked in his apartment. He doesn't trust anyone. He is a very violent man, even before Bernelli died. They really do not have an answer why."

"Warren does."

"How is that?"

"I don't know when, but Warren is going to Florence. He is determined to set things right. I believe he has a plan."

"Really. Without leaving his bed. That's impressive."

"He has his moments, Joseph. If you hear anything, let me know. Give my love to Luca."

"I will. Talk later."

Allen called soon after. "Hi, Allen, how are you?"

"I'm good. They pulled the guard from Warren's room. They believe there is no risk at this time."

"I agree. It's been three weeks."

"He will be coming home soon. Maybe that will put him in a better mood."

"I hope so. Have you set a date on the wedding?"

"Not yet. Warren's looking over brochures for the reception and I am shopping."

"That's good. Anyway, I have to go. I wanted to keep you updated."

"Thanks Allen. Bye."

Warren was released from the hospital two days later. Allen and Henry stopped by the house for a visit. Surprisingly, they all became good friends. Henry's wife made a pot of stew, and Allen brought bread and wine.

This was Warren's first glass in over a month. He took his time to savor the wine, then they ate. They discussed the wedding and the plans they kept changing.

Warren asked Shelly if she could introduce Allen to one her friends.

Allen groaned. Embarrassed, he said, "Please, Shelly, I am dating. Not serious but dating."

"If you change your mind...." They touched wine glasses.

Henry said his goodbyes after dinner. "I enjoyed the company but must return home to my family. Warren, take care. I am glad your home."

"Thank you, Henry." Shelly kissed his cheek and said she would talk to him later.

"Allen," Warren said quietly, "I have...." He paused. Shelly almost choked on her wine.

Allen put his hands over his face. "No, don't tell me."

Shelly asked. "What, Allen?"

"You're going to Italy. I knew it. I told Henry this morning you would not be that crazy. Shelly, What's wrong with you? You're as nuts as he is. Why would you agree to this? Bezos is mad, and dangerous."

"I'm sorry, Allen. I had to tell you." Warren felt guilty, but he needed to explain. "Shelly wants to go, and I need to."

"Revenge Warren?"

"No, not revenge. Pay back. Bezos did not have to shoot. He was told by his men; I was not Crawley. He enjoyed it."

"Pay back!"

"I promise I won't go anywhere near Bezos. Shelly will be with me all the time. She is pretty unhappy with Bezos as well."

"Say you go to Florence and come up with a plan. How do you expect to successfully pull this off, the two of you?"

Shelly said they have a friend.

"All right, three. You are all crazy."

"Allen, we will be back in a week. All of this will go away."

"One condition."

"What's the condition?"

"I have a friend in Florence; you call him when you are settled."

"I promise." She kissed his cheek.

Warren held out his hand. They shook on it.

"When will you be leaving?"

"Tomorrow."

30

Florence

Not wanting to draw attention to themselves, they departed from Dulles Airport and changed their flight in Paris. From there they flew to Rome. They rode a train to Florence.

It was a hard trip for Warren. He needed rest and his wound was bothering him. At the hotel, Shelly helped him to bed and went down to the lobby.

Joseph was waiting for her. They hugged and he asked how Warren was.

"He's in bed. The trip was too much for him. Hopefully, he will sleep all night."

Someone tapped her shoulder. "Luca!" she yelled. "Oh, it is so good to see you. I can't believe you came."

"Joseph and I discussed this and decided we would help. I couldn't sit at home alone, not with you three doing whatever you do."

"I'm glad. Putting each on an arm. Let's go find a bar and catch up."

Warren slept all night and then some. At 11:00 a.m. he finally managed to make it for a late breakfast. He gave Shelly a kiss and sat for some eggs and toast, coffee and orange juice and two cups of water.

"When can we expect Joseph?"

"Around noon. I had a drink with him last night."

"Really?"

"Yes, really. We didn't want to wake you. Are you feeling better?"

"Much better. I need a shower. I'll be back in a little."

Warren decided he did not want to leave the shower. The water was therapeutic, as hot as he could stand it. It wasn't until he heard Shelly yelling from the other room that he turned the water off and dried himself. A quick shave and a change of clothing, he was back to normal. Joseph was on the couch when Warren came into the room. He stood to shake his hand.

"You look good for almost being dead."

"Joseph! Christ."

Warren turned to where the voice came from. "Luca, what are you doing here?"

"Hi, to you also. Give me a hug. Good to have you back."

"Thank you."

"I thought you might need my help. Can't expect you and Shelly to do this alone. Can you?"

"Welcome to our little project."

"By the way, we are going to have company," Joseph announced.

Warren asked. "Who is that?"

"You'll see in a few minutes."

Warren asked Shelly.

She just shrugged.

They made room for Warren to sit. They noticed he was still hurting.

"Too soon, Warren," Luca said. She wrapped a blanket around him.

There was a knock on the door. Suddenly, everyone had a gun pointing at the door.

"Where's mine?" Warren wanted to know.

"Quiet," Shelly whispered.

Joseph opened the door slowly and in walked a very tall, very pretty blonde, smiling.

"Hi, everyone." Luca went over to hug her, then Joseph.

Shelly and Warren exchanged glances. Warren thought he recognized her but couldn't remember.

She walked over to where Warren was. "Don't get up, Warren, you're hurt. Hi Shelly, I'm Greta."

"Hello, I'm sorry, have we met?"

"Not formally. We met in Germany."

Warren remembered. "Van Dyne."

"Yes, Greta Van Dyne. Good memory."

Shelly was still staring at the woman. "Mrs. Van Dyne?"

"I was. He is deceased."

Shelly sat beside Warren and held his hand. "I'm sorry."

"Don't be. I'm not. That's why I'm here."

Warren said, "I don't understand, Greta. Here for what?"

She turned. "Joseph dear, can you explain? That would be better."

"In Germany, at the scene of the accident, Greta saw Shelly and I pull Warren away, and then Shelly helped Greta and her friend. She also saw me at the hospital with both of you. Greta had come to our jewelry store a few times, so she knew who I was, and Luca. She asked about Warren's injuries, then Crawley, and asked how we knew you. A few weeks later she asked more questions and somehow deduced you had something to do with the accident. I assured her you didn't. Two days later I told her you had been shot at home and were in the hospital, she asked if she could help."

Warren listened to Joseph's story carefully and then asked, "Greta, if you thought I had anything to do with your husbands' death, why help me?"

She sat across from Shelly but looked directly at Warren. My husband, late husband was not a good man. He was violent and possessive. He took his anger and his troubles out on me, so there was very little love between us."

Shelly said she was sorry.

"Thank you, Shelly."

"You saved my life, Warren, from the accident and my husband. If I can help, let me."

"What made you believe Warren had anything to do with the accident if the police said otherwise?" Shelly asked.

"Carl always suspected Joseph was police or government, but he couldn't prove it. He and his wife owned the shop, and they were friendly with the townspeople. I told him he was being paranoid, but I thought you were, Joseph. A feeling, that's all. I never said anything to Carl. When I saw you with Warren, I was convinced."

There was another knock on the door. Warren put his hands up. "Why not?"

Joseph moved towards the door. "Anyone expecting?"

"No, no one."

"Let's do this." All the guns were pointed at the door again.

Joseph opened it, and Warren said, "It's all right. Come in Allen."

Shelly went over to him and gave him a big hug. "What brings you here?"

"I thought you would be alone, but it looks like a party."

Shelly turned to everyone. "Introductions are in order."

"Allen Day, this Joseph Faust."

"We spoke on the phone. Pleased to finally meet you."

"This is his wife Luca."

"Hi, Allen."

Greta walked up to him. "Hi, my name is Greta."

"How are you Greta?"

"I'm well, thank you."

Everyone pulled up a seat around the table. Shelly and Luca poured wine for everyone.

Warren opened up with, "Allen is my supervisor at work. He knows more about law enforcement than I ever could."

"You are government? All of you?" Greta asked.

Shelly answered that one. "CIA," and then pointing to Joseph and Luca, "German."

"I wasn't aware you worked together like this."

Warren grinned. "We don't."

She looked confused.

Allen helped. "Greta this is not official."

"Oh. I understand."

"I forgot to mention something, Allen. This is Greta Van Dyne."

He looked stunned. "Van Dyne as in Germany?"

"Yes, she has offered to help. Acceptable?"

"If all of you agree...? Yes."

"Good. Greta, you're part of the team." She smiled at Warren.

She whispered, "Thank you."

"Shall we begin?"

31

Planning the Plan

Warren and Shelly sat on the sofa with Greta. Allen was beside her, and Joseph and Luca across from Warren.

"I want to thank all of you for being here. From the start, I thought it would be Shelly and me, like it's always been. With six of us, I will have to rework a few things. Same idea, same outcome. It's obvious I cannot move too far or fast, so I will have to rely on you all to be my eyes. Like all of our other assignments, we gather data and information. The risk is lowered and much easier to resolve any problems that occur. There is never irrelevant data. By the way, Greta, I am an analyst working for the CIA. That's what I do. This is a side job."

"It's a hell of a side job, Warren." They all laughed.

"Besides studying everything and everyone, I will need ideas and suggestions. Always. Here is the thing. We can either get this done quickly and quietly to ensure results, or...."

"What's that, Warren?" Shelly was rubbing his hand, thinking he was back to his old self.

"We can... stretch this out and have some fun."

Luca was startled. "Have some fun. You are trying to kill someone."

"No, I'm not."

"Then why are we here?"

Allen was watching this play out, then jumped in. "What do you mean, not?"

All eyes were on Warren.

"Accidental accident. He will do it himself."

"Why would Bezos kill himself?" Joseph asked.

Warren said, "He won't kill himself; he will accidently get in an accident."

Shelly said, "I love you Warren, but this crazy talk."

Greta asked, "Warren when my husband died, did you plan the accident?"

"Yes and no, Greta."

"Please explain."

Warren thought he owed her an explanation.

"I set it up, Greta. I set it in motion. I anticipated certain moves by either the persons involved, the cart, wagon, even the awning. I did set it up, but I had to rely on everything falling into place. There was only a small window of opportunity to work with. The cart hit the post and then the Mercedes. Everyone's reaction to that contributed to the chaos. By you screaming, you set things in motion. The driver outside his car, all the attention was drawn to him, and once panic sets in, people, most people, tend to overreact and not see the obvious. It may not explain it all, but it's hard to put in perspective."

"That is incredible, Warren. All that in five minutes." Greta was speechless.

Shelly smiled at Greta. "It's his way of thinking. Normal people don't think like that. He thinks of games and puzzles."

Greta laughed. Everyone was impressed by Warren's explanation but would never fully understand.

Shelly told Warren to continue.

"Thank you." He winked at her. "All the intel we have received confirms what we thought. Bezos is unstable, unpredictable, and insecure. He is becoming more violent and increasingly paranoid. He is always sure someone is challenging his position in the world. His partner, a Mr. Bernelli was in an accident and died six months ago." Greta looked at Warren and raised her eyebrows.

"Yes, Greta." She grinned.

"With Bernelli gone, it created a vacuum of power. He is concerned about that, also his temperament. That's why he came after me. He believed he was next. He was wrong. We had not heard of him. He still believes it to be true. Plus, I am still alive. I can't kill anyone. Not with a gun or a knife. It's not who I am, but because I do computers and puzzles, we can play a hell of a game. Do you want to play?"

"Let's do the game, Warren." Greta tried to hold back her excitement.

"How long, Allen asked, "will this take?"

"A week or two."

"I don't know about you, but this is quite expensive, meaning the hotel." Luca was ready to respond, but Greta beat her to it.

"Don't anyone worry about money. When my husband died, guess who inherited his estate? You cannot imagine how much he was worth. I didn't even know. I will stop by the desk and put it all on my account."

"Are you sure, Greta?" Luca asked.

"Yes, dear. I'm sure."

"Thank you, Greta." Shelly got up to hug her.

"Is everyone in? Allen?"

"Yes, I'm in."

"Joseph and Luca?"

"Yes," Luca answered.

"Shelly?"

"Of course, but if it doesn't work, I will get you." They raised their glasses.

Greta stood. "All right, you boys have your talk. The girls and I are going shopping, then we are going to do lunch."

"Sounds great." Luca jumped up along with Shelly.

Warren stopped Shelly. "We need six burner phones."

"I'll get it." she kissed him goodbye. Luca kissed Joseph. They left. Joseph poured more wine.

"Allen," Warren asked, "are you all right with this?"

"I'm fine. Do you know what you are doing?"

"A little. We need sketches of the area and a lot more information. The girls will be helpful with that. Joseph, Luca will never be in a dangerous situation."

"Thank you, Warren."

"Lord knows how long they will be. Shopping with money."

Warren picked up the phone. "Let's order lunch, shall we?"

After lunch, Warren said he needed rest and asked them to come back around 7:00 p.m.

He lay on the bed and was asleep in no time.

Four hours later Shelly returned. He was surprised he had slept that long.

He went into the living room; Shelly was stretched out on the sofa. Warren sat with her and rubbed her back.

"Did you have fun?"

"We had so much fun. Germans are crazy. All we did is run around. I am so tired; I'll lie here for a while."

"You only have until 7:00. That's when everyone is coming over."

"All I need."

Warren sat at the table, writing. He had to decide what information he needed and who to send to get it.

He now had five other people to work with instead of him and Shelly. This will take some planning, he thought.

The most important was the layout of the apartment building Bezos was in. All the streets, alleys, and stores needed to be on paper so they could all see clearly. Warren would like to see in the building, but that seemed unlikely.

He woke Shelly.

"A little longer, Warren, Please."

"Unless you want a crowd watching you as you sleep, you better get moving."

"Don't care."

"Come on." He pulled her up to a sitting position. Her head was on his shoulders, her arms around his neck.

"You take a shower, and I will put on some coffee."

"I'm going. Bring me the coffee when it's finished."

He picked up the phone and called Greta.

"Hi, Warren. Anything wrong?"

"No, We, are all meeting at 7:00. Can you make it?"

"I'll be there."

The knocking on the door brought Shelly out of the bedroom. "Already?"

"Here we go."

Warren and Shelly made coffee. Seemed like they all needed it.

Shelly passed around the burner phones. "Numbers are already down-loaded so we can keep in touch."

Greta was on the room phone. She was speaking Italian, so no one had any idea what was said.

Noticing everyone watching her, she said, "What? I ordered wine for the night. Good Italian wine."

"Italian and German?" Allen asked.

"And French, English and a little Spanish." Greta smiled at him. "You should learn some Allen."

They all waited for the wine, so there would be no interruptions. Then the planning commenced.

32
Coming Together

When the coffee was finished, wine was poured.

"If we continue like this for two more weeks," Allen joked, "we will be a mess."

"This is Italy, Allen. Enjoy." Greta was having fun and she was obviously flirting with Allen.

He didn't seem to mind. She was intelligent, beautiful, and very wealthy.

Luca asked, "Warren what do you have in mind for tomorrow?"

Warren opened his notebook to the first page.

"Christ, Warren," Joseph said laughing. "How did you write so much? We haven't been here two days."

Shelly was laughing also. "Joseph, left alone outside for an hour; he would fill the book."

"It's just a few pages, guys. I have a list of places we have to visit. We will need drawings of the whole area. We'll do that later. All the streets, around the apartment, the alleys. We can't rely on maps. They don't show the nooks and crannies. When you are out, visit shops and restaurants, pick a direction. Allen, you and Greta go together. A couple can go to a lot more places than a single man or woman. Joseph and Luca, the same. Observe everything. If you have to write it down, do it, but, discreetly. Shelly will be out front. Have fun shopping and dining. You have the phones, so keep in touch. Not just me. You are all tourists. Take your time. When you leave in the morning let everyone know so we don't worry."

Shelly grabbed him. "What are you doing while we work?"

"I have to design a game."

"This is not a game, Warren," Allen said annoyed. Allen was trying to get through to him.

"It has to be, Allen. Otherwise it has no chance to succeed. Step by step, it has to fall into place."

Allen shook his head. "Shelly, help me out here."

"I can't, Allen. He has to think of this as a game. He understands the risks and the consequences if he fails. If you are building something to start a ripple effect or a chain reaction you have to think like he does. That's why you brought him into your program. Isn't it? How do you think all the other assignments succeeded?"

"Accidental accidents," Joseph threw out.

Warren looked surprised that Joseph remembered. "You are quite right, Joseph. Listen, I will always be honest with you and will answer all your questions. The important thing is no one gets hurt. We need sleep. Call me when you are leaving in the morning.

It was quiet. The room was empty except for Warren and Shelly. She laid her head on Warren's lap.

"I am so tired, Warren. All I want to do is sleep." She knew he was running the numbers through his head. Numbers, names, streets, and time. Especially time. Everything was important, everything was noted. Shelly loved when he was working on a project; he was a different person. He was alive and enjoying life. Boredom was his enemy.

They went into the bedroom and slept the night away.

33

Studying Florence

Warren received his first call at 7:00. Allen and Greta were heading west. Luca called at 7:30. She had heard from Allen, so they would go east. They will call back later. Shelly was still eating. She was on her second plate of eggs and sausage. Warren hoped in ten years she wouldn't gain a hundred pounds.

He got into the shower, then shaved. He had to have Shelly help with the bandages; she nagged him about changing them more often.

She called Allen and surprisingly Greta answered.

"Hi, Shelly, how are you?"

"I'm fine. What happened to Allen?"

"He's here; hold on."

"Hi, Allen. How is the morning coming along?"

"Good so far. I think we have hit every store. Greta is educating me on how to be Italian."

"She is German, Allen."

"But worldly. Thank God she speaks their language."

Shelly grinned, visualizing them like two teenagers on a date.

"Anything interesting?"

"We walked around the apartment complex. It's huge. There are at least six exits and it's blocked on two sides. I'll make a sketch later."

"Perfect. Thanks, Allen. By the way...."

"What's that?"

"Have fun."

"I will. Bye."

Joseph checked in. They were three blocks west in a small coffee shop. The Italians loved giving history lessons of the city. Florence was the beginning of the Renaissance period in art and architecture. The owner was more than happy to explain to foreigners about Italian ingenuity. "We may not get out of here."

"Thank you, Joseph. Call me later."

Shelly stood by Warren at the table. Blank papers were laid out, touching one another, covering the entire table.

"This will be our map," Warren said. "A city map does not show the details required for this little project of ours. When they return, we will have them sketch where they were and what they observed. Relevant or not."

She told Warren it was time to go to the lobby and watch Bezos's apartment. Their lobby sat directly across from his entrance, so the view will be just what she needed.

"I'll be back soon. Keep your phone close."

Allen and Greta sat eating Italian pastries on the patio of a small café. Only two blocks from the apartment they were able to enjoy each other's company, plus keep an eye on it.

Greta had not had this much fun for so long. She loved being with Luca and Shelly. Unexpected friends were always the best, she thought. Now, Allen, whom she had only just met, made her feel happy, and she finally, after so many years, felt good about herself. They were there, she understood, to help a man die. Her deceased husband did that for a living; it was no secret, and she was able to accept it. This man Bezos wanted to kill Warren for no reason, so she could justify helping.

Watching Allen, she was feeling young and silly. She smiled at the thought of dating again. This was not supposed to be a date, but they acted as if it was. He was always the gentleman, making sure she was safe and comfortable. He asked if she would like to visit another shop.

She reached for his hand, and he accepted it. She smiled as they walked slowly up and down the street.

From one of the lobby chairs by the window, Shelly had the perfect view of the apartments entrance. Without looking too obvious she read a magazine, peering over from time to time to see if there was anything unusual across the street.

Luca and Joseph stopped by to say hello on their way to the elevator.

Two hours passed and she decided to leave the lobby. She stopped by the restaurant to order sandwiches for the group. Allen and Greta were there, which surprised her. They must have come past while she was ordering the food.

They were all watching Joseph drawing an outline of the area east of the apartments. Luca was pointing to certain places on the map. He drew them in. Her memory seemed a little better than Joseph's.

"I didn't know you were an artist, Joseph," Warren said admiring his work.

"When I was younger, I had toyed with the idea of art school, but never followed through."

"Well, if Allen and Greta don't mind, I think we have our cartographer."

"We don't mind," they said in unison.

Luca pointed to another spot. "Warren, this is a path leading to an open area, like a plaza. There is a fountain off to the side here. Five large statues surround the plaza with benches in between. Maybe ten."

"How big or wide of an area do you think?"

"Twenty meters diagonally, not quite circular, but close. The paths criss-cross, one leads to a business section, the other into a main intersection. "

"What about the third?" Warren asked.

"We never made it that far. Sorry."

"No, no, don't be. This will work out fine. Allen, lightly draw what you remember. Joseph will work with you. Greta, help him. Any details will help."

It didn't take Joseph long at all to complete. Everyone was involved with bits of information. A change here, an addition, widen this. By dinner they had a map covering four blocks. Warren taped the papers together to make one large sheet. They stood back to admire their work. "That's wonderful work," Greta remarked. "I am so proud of us."

Shelly ran her fingers along the streets. "North, south and so on. It's almost professional," she said.

They cleaned the table off and placed trays of food out. Passed plates around and ate. Allen broke the silence.

"Guess what we have?" No one answered.

"We have wine. Italian."

The dinner was finished the table cleared, and Greta poured wine.

"A toast!" she shouted. "To friends. To friends." The celebration was still going on for a half hour.

Shelly went to Warren and put her arms around him. He was alone and quiet studying his notes and the map. "Give me a kiss." It suddenly got quiet at the table. "Give me a kiss. It's time." Now everyone's attention was on Shelly. He kissed her.

"What is this all about?" Luca asked.

Shelly moved to another chair near the table.

"It's time to share the plan."

Greta couldn't believe it. "Already? It has only been two days."

Shelly smiled at her. "Greta, he knew what he wanted to do in the hospital."

"Do you know?"

"No. He never said anything. I know Warren."

"What about all of our work, the map?" Luca looked crushed. They all looked disappointed.

Warren stood slowly, holding his chest. Shelly knew he was in pain, but he had to go through with this.

"Luca and Greta. Your help was needed. I cannot go out, and I definitely cannot move fast. This is only the first part of the plan. Two days, yes. It will take another week to bring it to an end. I've known what I wanted to do since the hospital, but I have never been to Florence. I did not know where Bezos lived or what kind of apartment he lived in. It could have been in a suburb. You have shown me the layout of this area. It didn't take me long to see the only way to get Bezos is for him to come to me. He needs to leave the apartment. It would have been pointless to attempt anything without information. It is similar to a game." He glanced at Allen. "You are all my friends, and I needed to have a back door to the plan so no one would be hurt.

"This is what we have to work with. Bezos is here," he said, pointing to the building. "We have to approach this logically. He doesn't have to leave; his security is good. At least ten I would guess. That is sufficient to hold off an army or anyone motivated to replace him.

"For the next few days, we have to convince him he is being tested and someone is coming for him. He will not know who, but he thinks everyone is out for him and his position of power so that will work in our favor."

"How is that, Warren?" Greta asked.

"Good question. People see what they want to see. In most cases it's harmless, but if you truly believe you are being challenged, even the smallest, most subtle thing out of the ordinary is automatically considered an assault or the possibility of one. Ultimately, what we have is someone on the edge and it is our job to push him over. That's when mistakes happen."

"And accidents," Joseph added.

"Most definitely. We are going to very subtly help him prove he is correct and that he is not paranoid as they all believe him to be. Although, he will be wrong."

"So where do we start, Warren?" Allen was trying to understand.

"We will schedule a series of small unconnected, timed events and situations, to have him overreact and try to connect them."

Warren looked at Luca. "Are you all right? No hurt feelings?"

"No, I understand."

"Good, I'm glad."

"It will increase the anxiousness in all of them. Piece by piece, we build momentum. Similar to the game Mouse Trap. Have you all heard of it?" They nodded yes. "Then, once it starts to move on its own there is no stopping it."

"What if he does not come out?" Joseph asked.

"Then we push a little harder."

Warren looked at Luca and Greta again. "The plan was easy once we had the map. Executing it will be fun. He saw Allen's face. Sorry, Allen. Wrong choice of words. Interesting...."

Shelly moved closer to the map. "Where do we start?"

Warren put his finger on the alley behind the apartments. "Right here."

"Allen, you said you have a friend here. Is he up for a little mischief?"

"I'll give him a call. What do you need?"

"We need a small fire."

Shelly said, "What? A fire."

"A little one, in the alley. Not too big. Enough to get their attention. He could leave once it's lit. When it starts, we will be surrounding the building to see what they do. We need to see how they react and how many men they send out. Also, it's very important to find out where Bezos's rooms are in the complex."

Greta laughed and said, "So, the fun begins." That made them all laugh.

"We will cover all the exits. Allen, if you can arrange that fire."

"When do you want it?"

"Tonight, would be good."

34

The Execution

At 9:30, Allen's friend created a splendid fire in the alley. Everyone was in place as arranged. Allen and Greta were close enough to see the entire alley, yet remained out of sight. They knelt on the grass, Greta had her arm around Allen, her head resting on his shoulder. He was not sure what his friend had used to ignite the fire in the dumpster, but it burned hot and bright. Within minutes the complex was lit and sounds from inside could be heard. The fire was far enough away from the apartment not to cause concern, however, the residents seemed to panic.

Lights were turned on, windows opened, and shouting was coming from everywhere. Police arrived and fire trucks backed into the alley. Men were scurrying with their hoses. Ten minutes later the fire was extinguished. Twenty minutes after that, the fire trucks left. The police looked around, behind cans and fences then they drove away.

Greta started to raise up, but Allen stopped her. He held her tight and said, "Shhh." He put his fingers over her mouth. "Look there." He pointed to the exit closer to them.

In the alley, two men were slowly searching the rear of the alley, behind the dumpster, and checked the other doors. They were obviously Bezos's guards. One had a gun in his hand hanging to his side. Satisfied, they went in and shut the door.

"Now we can go." He took Greta's hand, and they walked to the hotel.

It was close to 11:00 before they were in Warren's room.

Luca helped Shelly pour coffee while they briefed each other.

Joseph was first. "I was west of the building. I was able to see the light, but not the fire. Heard the police and fire trucks. From my position, not much action. Only one man came out, looked around, then went back inside."

Luca had very little activity. "I saw one man near the east end, but he didn't stick around long."

Allen and Greta both showed where they were and explained the events. "After the police left two men came out for around five minutes."

Shelly described how, as soon as the fire started, the lights in all the rooms were lit, on the third floor facing the hotel. Five minutes later a car pulled in front of the entrance.

"No one got out, and no one got in," she said. "The car left at 10:30."

"So, it seems that Bezos has a plan himself to evacuate. I'm hoping he saw this as a possible distraction or a warning."

Joseph was tracing the apartment with his finger. "Do you think Bezos is on the third floor?"

"My guess is yes."

"He is expecting something, isn't he?"

"I would say if nothing else, he will be on his guard," Allen replied.

"Allen and Joseph, I have a question. Is it possible to add a few passengers on a flight, ghosts; and on trains, from different places to Florence? All with very obvious fake names."

"For what, Warren?"

"I would assume a man in his position would have people and contacts stationed around airports and train stations. They would, I suspect, get in touch with Bezos. Imagine people all of a sudden are traveling to Florence with fake names. Hotels and bed and breakfasts too. No one has to be there, but they'll be expected. If he found out that all these people were coming here and staying around the corner, that would drive him crazy."

Greta smiled understanding the logic behind it. "They would believe they were there for them."

"Yes, they would. Everyone that passes by or is in the complex would be suspect."

"I would hate to be a delivery man," Joseph said, concerned. "What do you think?"

"Shall we try it?" All agreed. "Let's get some sleep. We'll talk more tomorrow."

The next morning Joseph and Allen called. Shelly answered. "Warren's changing his bandages. He will be a while."

"All the arrangements have been made in Washington and Berlin. The IT guys will come up with some interesting ideas and put it out there."

Shelly thanked them. "I'll tell Warren."

Warren was thrilled with the news. "I hope this works."

Shelly kissed him. "It will. Your friends believe in you."

"I know, it helps. I miss being with you alone. It is always very crowded."

"We will have time when this is over, and you are healthy."

"I hope so. Anyway, I have work now. What are you up to?"

"The girls and I are going shopping."

"Again?"

"Yes, again. I really enjoy being with them."

"I am glad you have fun. It's good for you, instead of taking care of me."

"I'm fine. You will be too. Don't get grumpy. I'll be back sometime this afternoon."

"Don't forget your phone."

"Got it. Love you."

Warren wasn't sure where Allen and Joseph were. With the girls gone, he worked for a short time, ate, and took a nap. This was a good day.

Shelly came back at 6:00. Bags of clothes hung from her arms.

"Do you have enough?"

"You ought to see what Luca and Greta bought. I was being good. I bought you something, my husband-to-be."

"What's that?"

She handed a bag to him. He pulled a T-shirt out. A black shirt with red and white letters. "Florence the Renaissance."

"I will stand out. It's beautiful."

"I'm glad you like it."

"I have a question, Shelly."

"Yes?"

"What does Greta say about Allen?"

Shelly gave him a look.

"Why?"

"Curious."

"Well, she is madly in love with him. Can't stop talking about him. I don't think she has ever been in love. Or has been loved."

"I would say Allen feels the same."

"Is that what you asked?"

"Yes. I have something I need done today."

"Like what?"

"Hold on." He picked up the phone.

"Allen, Hi. Do you have any plans tonight?"

"No, not at all. What do you need?"

"How would you like a trip to the country?"

"The country?"

"Bezos has a house about fifty miles from here. It may be beneficial to us if we could get the layout and how it is set up. See if Greta can go. She knows the language and can keep you company.

Allen paused for a moment. "All right, I'll give her a call."

"Thanks, Allen. I'll text you the address.

Shelly stood looking at him. "Warren."

"Yes?"

"I cannot believe you are doing this."

"I need the place checked out."

"I could have gone."

"Yes, you could, but this is going to be fun."

"You are so bad, you know that?"

"They need a chance to be alone. There is always someone with them. They are too embarrassed to spend the night together here. So, I'll help them."

"I love you. Thank you for thinking of them."

"You are welcome. Now kiss the kind man."

Allen and Greta rented a car, and with help from the GPS they sped off to the country. The drove an hour before they found the house. It looked empty. No lights were on and the front gate was open. Woods were in the rear of the house, and on the sides were other houses. It was 9:00, and Allen thought it would be too late to stay and watch.

He called Warren and told him about the house. Warren agreed. "Find a place to stay the night and check in the morning when it's light."

They found a bed and breakfast, paid for the room. It only took one minute before they were undressed and on the bed.

In the morning they drank coffee in bed.

"Allen, you describe Warren as a computer man, a loner. Look what he does for Shelly. Look what he is doing with Bezos. I would say your file on him is wrong. He is brilliant and clever, but he is great with people. Very observant."

"I don't know. That's how I always saw him. How everyone saw him."

"He is also very wise and unpredictable."

"Why do you say that?"

"Look at us. We are here alone. It was difficult in the hotel, so he set this up. He knew."

"You may be right." He thought for a while. "Yes, you may be right."

There was nothing at the house, so they headed back to Florence. By noon they were all seated eating lunch.

Warren got up to lock the door. Greta came up from behind hugged and kissed him. "Thank you, my friend."

Shelly raised her eyebrows questioningly.

Warren shrugged.

"We know there is nothing at Bezos house in the country. Allen and Greta surveyed the place this morning. It doesn't look like he has any intentions of going back. That's good news."

"By the way, Allen, can you get in touch with your friend. This time we need two men."

"I'll call. Why two?"

"Look at the map. We need a distraction here, but I'm not sure what."

"How big?" Joseph asked.

"Big enough for them to send their car around."

Luca suggested a few broken windows. "Not his, but well placed."

"That will work. Great."

"What about the second one, Warren?" Shelly asked.

"I think a car crash is in order."

"Are you serious?" Allen was not sure about this.

"Just a small accident. Bezos will, if he was smart, think it was aiming for him. Stir some things up, so to speak. I don't want your friends to get hurt or compromised. Speak to your friends, maybe they have some ideas as well. After this we will need some more situations to put them through. Tell them to try to set it up tomorrow. Make sure they give us the time."

Greta asked if she could speak.

"Anytime," Shelly told her.

"You all know I was married to Carl for ten years. There was no love between us. I was not involved in anything, no friends or family. I'm not complaining, it was my decision. If it had not been for Shelly and Warren I would still be married and somehow those events brought me here." She had to take a drink of coffee. She continued slowly. "This is the first time I am part of a family. To be included. I have been so happy this week. It's so exciting to have a purpose and to have loving friends. I wanted you to know how I feel." She was crying hard; Shelly and Luca wrapped their arms around her. Then she stopped and said, "Even though someone is going to die."

They all burst out laughing.

Joseph stood. "Anyone for going to the bar?"

All at once: "Yes!!"

The next evening everything was set. All the exits were covered, and Warren and Shelly were in the lobby watching the front entrance of the apartment. Warren was hurting but wanted to see for himself what would happen. Allen briefed them on what his friends suggested. They decided not to go for the windows but to break into the rear door. Perhaps if there was time, try an interior door. They thought that would be more effective.

It was.

Ten minutes later a black car pulled alongside the apartments. Two men sat in the front. The engine was running as they waited. No one exited the building. Warren thought the plan failed. The door at the front entrance suddenly opened and two men ran to the car and jumped in.

"Bezos," Shelly cried out. Warren agreed. He called Allen.

"Anything?"

"Yes, Men everywhere. They are inspecting the door. Searching in and outside. They are very nervous."

"Stay hidden. If they get close, leave."

"I will."

Joseph and Luca confirmed the activity from where they sat.

Warren was worried Bezos would drive off.

The car door opened, and Bezos returned to the apartment.

"His men must have called him," Shelly said.

They saw a car moving from the west. It was an old Renault. It swerved to the side and slammed into the rear of the waiting car. There were people gathering around. The drivers were cursing in Italian at each other. The police arrived and separated them.

No one was injured. The driver explained his tire had blown, and he lost control. He apologized over and over. He was given a violation, and the tow truck arrived to carry it away.

The street settled down. Bezos's car had little damage done to it considering the sound it created. They drove away under their own power.

Shelly made the calls to bring everyone in.

In the room Warren opened a bottle and passed it around. While everyone was discussing the crash, Warren wrote it all down in his book.

"I'm sorry I missed the crash. Was it exciting?" Allen asked.

"It was," Warren answered. "Even though we were expecting it, it caught us off guard. You friends have to be commended. That was brilliant."

"I'll let them know.

"We'll have to meet them when this is over. Explain why they are doing crazy things."

Luca touched Shelly's hand. "Do you think today helped us?"

"I don't know."

"I wish I could know something."

"Bezos might abandon the apartment. Bezos out of sight makes this significantly more difficult."

Joseph asked Warren, "What did you mean by pushing him?"

"We will have to bring him to us."

"Are you serious?"

"I am. I mentioned that before."

"To the hotel, Warren?" Greta asked.

"No, no. Someplace where we have control over the situation. Let's close for tonight. We'll talk tomorrow."

35
The Situation

In bed Shelly asked Warren, what was on his mind.

"Everyone is having a good time here in Florence. Falling in love, making new friends. Shopping." He smiled at her. A sense of belonging. "I feel guilty bringing Bezos into it. We are trying to kill someone, which, in itself is terrible. What effect will it have on our friends?"

"Warren, I know you don't like the idea of taking someone's life. That is why you make accidents. You don't get too close. You are always there when it happens, and you are responsible because you set it up, but only indirectly. You try to justify it in a way to not feel the pain."

Warren put his hands on his head. "I know. I am afraid to go too far; someone will get hurt. I couldn't live with that. It has always been just you to worry about. Now I have four more."

"Don't think about that, Warren. We will all be fine. The reason they are here to fall in love and to make friends, as you put it, is because you needed help. You didn't ask them to come. They came for you."

"That is not comforting. Now it makes it worse if someone gets hurt."

"No one will get hurt. Your plan is working."

"I hope I don't disappoint everyone. I have looked at this in different ways. Logically, if I calculated correctly, it should work. All of the evidence indicates Bezos is frightened. I am sure he's heard from his people about the flights from Washington, Berlin, and wherever the IT guys are bringing them in from. That should reinforce any delusions he might have. We are blind at the moment. We could be absolutely wrong. When you deal with a man that is unstable and irrational, he becomes unpredictable. I might be overthinking the whole game."

"You're tired and you are in pain. Let's get some sleep. Tomorrow you can ask everyone how they feel."

"I am tired." Shelly kissed him.

"Say good night, Warren."

"Good night."

In the morning, Shelly showered and had her breakfast. Warren said he felt better, but she worried about him.

"You need to eat."

"I will. I'll have coffee first."

They talked for a while, then she had to force feed him. He grudgingly ate some eggs and toast. He was more interested in the map. She had questions but decided to keep them to herself.

He put the map on the table. "Okay, I'm finished. I'll clean up and change the dressing, then we will gather our friends." He left the room.

Shelly sat there amazed. Looking at the map, there were no notes or markings that she could see that would indicate where he was going with this.

Shelly called Allen and Joseph. She asked if they could drop by in an hour.

Allen and Greta arrived first. They no longer were embarrassed sleeping in the same room. They were now an official couple.

Joseph and Luca came in a few minutes later. They looked well rested but carried with them their own cup of coffee.

Warren was seated at the table. The map was on the table in front of him. Shelly was beside him. "Good morning all. Sleep well?"

Luca yawned. "Yes. I feel great."

"Does anyone need food or drink?"

Greta asked for coffee and a glass of water. She went to the sink. Poured water, drank it down, and refilled it. Shelly handed her the coffee.

"Thank you, Shelly."

"I thought about this all morning," Warren started. "I think today we will enjoy Florence and not work at all."

"Are you sure?" Joseph asked. "There is still a lot we can do."

"I want to see if the work the IT guys did is affecting Bezos. I want to give it time to sink in, and that means we have a day off. What do you think, Luca?"

"I think it's great. Joseph and I can do some sightseeing. We haven't had a chance to see anything."

"Allen?"

Allen looked at Greta. "I am pretty sure we can find something to keep us occupied."

"I'm sure you can."

"I will, of course, be here, so if you need anything, give me a call."

They all looked around, not sure what to say. Warren saw the reluctance to leave in their faces.

"Seriously, go out and have fun. We will see you later."

"Okay." Luca gave Shelly a goodbye hug and they left the room.

Shelly remained in her seat after they had left. Warren moved to the sofa and put his feet up on a chair close by. No one said a word. Shelly was completely baffled at the change in Warren's plans. Today, they were to continue with pressuring Bezos in hopes he would make a mistake. The five of them had intended spending the day surveying the neighborhood and watching the apartment. They were looking forward to starting another fire or something. Now, nothing.

Warren held out his hand. Shelly took it and sat leaning on him. He ran his fingers through her hair and down her face. She leaned farther back, relaxing. She loved being touched by him. It was not sexual, it was love. His fingers played with her hair and on her neck. She had already forgotten what was on her mind at the table.

"You know, Shelly, when we are married, we'll have time to do whatever we want. Traveling would be decided by us and not others. That would be nice, don't you think?"

"That would be nice. To spend time with you alone."

"I have decided to resign when we return. Not because of getting shot, or Bezos, or even the danger, but to try something different."

Shelly moved her head, so she could see Warren's face. "What is the matter? Why are you thinking about resigning and marriage?"

"Honestly, I like the idea of getting married. We do well together outside the normal everyday way of living. Which means you will have to resign too. It would drive me crazy if you were in the field without me."

"What would I do?"

"We find work together. Start a business. It doesn't matter."

"Are you sure you're all right?"

"I am. Just thinking ahead. We'll be out of here in three days. Then what?"

"Three days?"

"Actually, we will resolve this tomorrow, but I figured we'd hang around for two more."

"You really do know how to finish this?"

"Yes. Let's take a nap."

"Now?"

"Come lay with me in the other room. It feels nice by your side."

The rest of the day they sat, ate, watched television, and slept. Shelly had a wonderful day alone with Warren. No company or phone calls. Just the two of them. Shelly did make calls to Allen and Joseph for them to all meet at 9:00 tomorrow, but that was it. They went to bed around 9:00 and surprisingly slept until 6:30 the next morning.

While getting ready, Warren explained why he told everyone to take a day off.

"We needed it for one, but also, we do this today and I wanted to be rested. The break was nice."

Shelly agreed. "It was nice. So, we're ready?"

"Time to work."

By the time company came they were rested, clean, and fed. No one complained about the day off. They enjoyed being tourists. Coffee was passed around by Shelly and Greta. Warren sat the table and asked them all to gather around.

Shelly told them they were drawing Bezos out of the apartment today.

Greta, who was beside her asked, "How?"

"I'll let Warren explain."

Warren put his finger on the map, centered on the apartment. "If I am correct in assuming Bezos has the third floor facing our hotel, I should be able to get his attention."

"You are not going out, are you?" Joseph asked, concerned about his health.

"I have to, Joseph. We need to push a little. I am afraid he will either leave or something unexpected will happen and waste the time we put into this. He doesn't know we are here. It wouldn't be safe if he knew, so we need him where we control the situation."

Luca put her hand on his. "Please, Warren, there has to be another way."

"I'm sure there is, Luca, but I have gone over this again and again. If he takes the bait, it will work."

Allen said, "Shelly talk to him."

Warren interrupted. "Allen, Shelly will be with me. I have no intention of getting in a fight. I won't be near him."

"I won't leave him," Shelly finally said.

"First thing. No guns. Leave them here. If the police come, as I plan, we are not official so we can be arrested if it goes bad. I don't believe it will, though. Bezos will have one. We have to be far enough away so he can't use it. This starts and ends at the plaza. I will bring him to you."

"Do you know how?" Allen asked.

"Oh, yes."

Warren explained everyone's position in the plaza and what they were to do. At 4:00 they would meet there.

"Eat, sleep, whatever you want. We have until then."

36

The Push

Warren wore his new T-shirt Shelly picked up a week ago. All black except for the red and white lettering. He would stand out anywhere. He sat on a bench in front of the hotel, directly across from the apartments. He had a clear view of the third floor, and they had one of him. Shelly was close by in case he had to move quickly.

This afternoon he had her tighten the bandages around his chest so he wouldn't injure himself any more than necessary.

Time went slowly. He stared at the windows above him waiting for any movement at all. A half hour went by. Then he saw a curtain move to the side. He sat still just staring at whoever was watching.

On the third floor a man was peering through an opening in the curtains. He had been watching the man on the bench for a while.

"Hey, boss," he called to the other room.

"What is it?"

"There is a man sitting across the street. He's been there about an hour."

"So, he's sitting. What else is he doing?"

"Nothing, just watching us."

"Do you know him?"

"Never saw him before."

Bezos walked to the curtain and looked out. He jumped to the side behind the wall.

His man did the same.

Bezos said, "That's him."

"Who's him?"

"Crawley, or Maypoole. The guy from Washington."

Bezos edged closer for a better view. He saw Warren looking up at the window.

Warren looked alone. Bezos saw another man standing below looking at the entrance to his apartment building.

"That's him. I know it."

"I wasn't in Washington. I never saw him," the man said. "I thought you killed him."

"So did I. Why is he here?" Bezos saw a woman looking up. "Who is that?"

"I don't know. Just some woman. There is nothing there, boss, to worry about."

"What do you think he is doing?"

"Do you want me to send someone down to look around?"

"Yes. Do that now."

Warren sensed he was there long enough, so he stood and walked to the plaza. Shelly walked the same direction keeping a distance between them. He was sure Bezos was watching him. The door to the apartments opened. A man came out and looked around. He walked the length of the sidewalk, both ends before he went inside.

"Hey, boss, nothing suspicious that I could see. Nothing out of the ordinary."

Bezos lost Warren. He opened the window and stretched his body to get a good look.

He spotted him. Warren was near the end of the block by the plaza. Warren was watching him. He saw Warren wave to him.

"He is trying to get me."

"He is only one man."

"He has friends in Washington. Remember they were flying in this week. How about Germany? How many are there?"

"I haven't seen any of them."

"The car crash, the fire. Even my own friends want me dead. I have to worry about them, now I have this man coming for me. We have to stop this. Who else wants me? We have to go out."

"Boss, I don't know about this. It looks like a setup to me."

Bezos screamed at him. "We cannot stay in here forever. It has to end, now."

Warren wished he knew what Bezos was up to. The curtains closed, but what did that mean. It didn't take long for the answer.

Bezos and two men walked out onto the street. The two men had their hands inside their coat pockets. Bezos was obviously nervous. His head was moving rapidly from side to side. The crowd of people had to dodge the men standing in the center of the sidewalk. Bezos thought they all were staring at him. A young woman stopped and reached into her handbag. When her hand came out, Bezos pulled his gun.

"Boss," said one of his men, "it's nothing." He grabbed his hand. The woman held her phone.

"Jesus, boss. This is crazy."

Bezos crossed the street and the two men followed. He stopped at the edge of the plaza.

"Where is he? Where is everyone?"

The two men separated but kept an eye on Bezos.

"Where are you Maypoole? Who are you working for?"

Warren came out of the bushes on the opposite side of the plaza.

"Hi Francis," He called out.

Bezos pulled his gun and aimed it at Warren.

Shelly thought he would fire. She was ready to pull Warren to safety.

From the left a man on a bench said something. Bezos turned, saw the man open a newspaper. Bezos pointed the gun at him.

"Boss, stop," one of his bodyguards yelled.

The paper was empty. When he looked back, Warren was gone.

A woman with a baby carriage was walking close by. She stopped suddenly and reached inside the carriage and brought out a bag.

Bezos yelled, "Stop!" He raised his gun. The woman screamed and dropped the bag. She pulled the carriage behind the fountain. The two men had their guns out pointing at everyone. Allen moved from behind a statue, when Bezos saw him, he moved back. Joseph on the other side did the same.

Bezos was yelling. Come out all of you. You are all dead. He was walking back and forth in the center of the plaza swinging his gun wildly.

Police cars were pulling in the plaza. The officers jumped out with their guns drawn. Stop put down your guns. It was all spoken in Italian, but it was clear to Warren what was said.

Bezos's men didn't know what to do. Bezos was still running around waving his gun.

"Put your guns down," the policeman yelled.

"They are not police," Bezos said.

"Boss, they are police." The men dropped the guns and raised their hands.

Luca walked from behind a statue at the same time Joseph stepped out from his. They passed by each other in the middle and looked at Bezos until they made it to another one.

Bezos yelled, "Stop! I will get all of you."

Allen poked his head out, looked at him then back. He did this three times. Greta walked out from behind the fountain and froze. Bezos pointed the gun at her, and she screamed loud. He was yelling at her to shut up. Someone else screamed. Shelly popped up from a bush. She too screamed.

Bezos continued to curse. Luca joined in. She was yelling and screaming. Suddenly everyone was running.

Bezos fired his gun and hit a statue. Greta and Luca dove behind the fountain. He fired again. This time at Joseph. It missed him.

By this time the police had enough. Bezos was a powerful man in town, but this was too much. "Drop the gun, Bezos, or we will shoot."

"I can't there are too many."

Warren came out of the bushes. "It's over, Bezos. Give it up. In English."

"No, you're not getting me." He ran. He took off across the plaza, the police ran after him. He ran past Allen and Greta not seeing them.

Bezos ran out into the busy intersection. A bus passed by, just missing him.

He raised his hands. "See, your plan didn't work. It missed." Bezos never saw the car coming from the other direction. The car hit him in the back, flipped him over into the windshield, then on to the ground. He died instantly.

Cars were stopped, and the police were trying to control the crowd. The two men were put into handcuffs and taken to a police car. Witnesses were gathered for reports.

Shelly helped Warren stand and quickly moved away from the plaza. Joseph and Luca left in another direction, then turned towards the hotel. Greta said she wanted to watch. She and Allen found a bench not far from the action.

37

Rest

It was 6:00, and they were all seated at the table.

"How do you feel Warren? Much pain?" Allen asked.

"Yes, but that's all right. I can rest later. That was a long two hours."

Shelly was holding him close to her.

Luca came over to Shelly. "That was the most amazing and crazy-ass thing I ever saw. I had no idea what was going on. Joseph and I were just coming up with ideas. We didn't know how long it would take."

"I'll say this, Warren. No one would ever believe we pulled this off." Allen was smiling.

Greta stood then walked over to Warren on the couch. She gave him a long hug and kissed his cheek.

When she was back at the table she said, "When I stood up and Bezos aimed that gun at me, I almost peed my pants. I just froze. It didn't last long; I knew I had my part to play. So, I screamed as loud as I could. Then everyone screamed. It was crazy. Poor Bezos was shattered. I bet he wanted to scream too."

They all laughed.

"Let's go to the bar." Warren stood. "We all deserve it."

38

To Friends

They were seated at a table at the bar in the hotel. Warren and Shelly ordered scotch, the rest wine. Everyone was happy it was over but agreed they would miss it.

A man in a suit stood beside Warren.

"Mr. Maypoole?"

"Yes."

"I am Inspector Galini. May I have a word, please?"

Joseph started to speak. Warren stopped him. "It's all right, Joseph."

Shelly helped Warren up and to a table against the wall. They waited until Shelly had left to talk.

"Mr. Maypoole, I made some inquiries. The hospital told me you were released yesterday. It would have been impossible for you to have been here all week."

"That would be difficult, Inspector."

"I can see that. Our Mr. Bezos is the man who shot you."

"Yes, he was."

"So, you came to talk to him."

"That's about it. I never had the chance."

"That was a terrible accident. Was it not?"

"That's what I heard from the guests here."

"Mr. Bezos was not a good man, and most here in Florence will not miss him. I guess we can thank whoever contributed to his demise. Although he had many friends, I can assure you that this was an unfortunate accident and your name will never be mentioned."

"Thank you, Inspector."

"Let me help you up." Shelly ran over to help.

"You enjoy the rest of your vacation. Stay as long as you like." Warren held out his hand. The Inspector obliged and shook. "Good day, sir, madam.

When they were back at the table, Allen asked what he wanted.

"For us to enjoy his city and stay as long as we like."

"Seriously?"

"Definitely."

They raised their glasses. "Toast.""

Luca asked Warren, "Did you anticipate the outcome?

"Not Really. With accidental accidents there are too many variables. We had to rely on Bezos, his bodyguards, and the police. Then you factor in the ordinary people. All of you were magnificent out there. The pace was perfect. He couldn't let his guard down for a minute.

Shelly said, "It happened so fast. Bezos was panicking, trying to understand. we were lucky his guards had the sense to see there was no threat and kept their guns lowered."

Warren thought for a moment. "With all the noise and commotion, police and people running everywhere something had to happen. We set it in motion. The rest came naturally. It's how people react to situations that cause the chaos. If you are Bezos and, in the middle, what do you do? He wanted to control but was not able to, so he used his gun. Thankfully only twice. That's when he ran. He needed space and time to think. He thought the bus was for him and it missed. The car didn't."

Joseph remembered what Shelly once said. It's always the second one.

"He could have been shot by the police. I think they were afraid to. He was a powerful man in Florence. His guards could have shot him, or someone else with a gun. You can never tell what will happen. Cause and effect. Whatever you want to call it. Same result."

Luca said, "You know, Warren, that was brilliant. It was all brilliant."

"Thank you. I could not even come close if you all were not here to help. I thank you. Toast." Warren kissed Shelly. "I love you."

"I love you."

After a few more drinks and toasts, Greta stood.

"Okay, the last toast. I am getting drunk here. As I said before, this has been the best and most exciting time in my life. I could never thank you enough, Warren. You saved me, then you gave me life. You gave me Allen. She blew Allen a kiss. You gave me a family I never had. I am forever grateful. Shelly and Luca, you are my sisters. I love you both. Joseph, you will always be my brother. Before I ramble on, let's toast to family and friends. Here, Here."

Shelly and Luca got up to hug Greta. She was crying again.

Greta asked. "Is anyone in a hurry to go home?"

They just looked at her.

"Come home with me. I have a large house in the mountains. We all can relax, and Warren can get healthy. I want to share something with you."

"Allen," Warren asked, "how are Davis and Matthews taking all of this? Have you spoken to them?"

"I've resigned."

"Are you sure you want to do that?"

"This time with all of you has shown, there is much more than being in an office. I actually had fun and made good friends."

"You are a good friend."

"I doubted you at first, to be honest. You are crazy and very clever. I won't do that again."

"And Greta?"

"Oh my God. I am crazy in love with her, and I have you to thank."

"Me?"

"You knew what you were doing. So did Shelly."

"Well, maybe a little."

"Can I offer some advice?"

"Of Course, anything."

"Marry that poor girl you are dragging around."

Warren smiled. "As soon as I can. Believe me."

Greta came over to Shelly. "May I borrow your husband?"

"He is not my husband yet." Shelly laughed. "Yes, you may."

"Come here, Warren." Greta helped him up, and they moved to the other table.

"What's the matter, Greta?"

She hesitated then rolled her eyes.

"What?"

"Do you think it is too soon to be madly in love after only a little over a week?"

"Greta, you are intelligent, beautiful, and fun to be around. Please love Allen with all your heart."

"Are you sure? And Allen?"

"He is crazy in love with you. His words. You deserve this. So does Allen. What's not to love about you?"

"No one has before," she said sadly.

"You have been waiting for the right man. That's all."

"Thank you, Warren. I am happy."

"Tell him."

"I will. I will, Warren." She kissed him and ran over to Allen.

Shelly came over and sat.

"Is she all right?"

"She is in love; I believe for the first time. She asked if it was too soon."

"And you said...?"

"Not even a little bit. I didn't tell her, but I loved you from the beginning."

"I did too. Was that too soon for us?" She kissed him.

"No, that was good for us."

"They do make a good couple. Are we going to Germany?" she asked. "It's not like we have other plans."

"Unless you call getting married plans."

"We will have time for that."

"Germany might be fun. We will get married soon enough."

"Deal. You get healthy first."

Warren grabbed her and held her tight. "I will be healthy soon. Don't worry."

He called for Luca.

"Yes, Warren?"

"I wanted to thank you personally. You were wonderful. A dear friend."

"Thank you. I would not have missed this for anything. An incredible two weeks. You and Shelly are the best friends I could have."

"Are you and Joseph going to Greta's?"

"Joseph said, 'Why not?' When I asked him."

"Good. This may be interesting."

The celebration lasted for a couple more hours. Greta was drunk. The others were close. Joseph and Warren spoke about Germany, then everyone went to their rooms.

Shelly and Warren were in bed planning their wedding when they get back to Washington.

Finally sleep came.

The End

Epilogue

Two weeks in Germany went too fast for Warren. He and Shelly spent hours in Greta's garden. Her house was larger than anything they had seen before. Over twenty rooms, a pool, and a game room. Probably a lot more that they haven't seen yet. It was easy to keep occupied. Warren was in heaven when he found Greta's kitchen. He was more than happy to cook dinners for everyone.

Joseph and Luca lived only a hundred miles from Greta, so they drove home for a few days and then returned.

Allen and Greta were never apart the whole time. They would go on long drives, spend hours in the pool, and lie on the sofa to watch bad television.

Near the end of their stay, Greta gathered everyone in the study.

"I have something to ask of you all. When I received my inheritance, I found that I owned a couple hundred acres of land, mostly in the mountains. The most beautiful scenery around. On that, there is a hunting lodge. A huge one, but it has not been used for years.

"While we were in Florence, I realized why I was having so much fun. It is because I found a purpose and a goal. It may sound silly, but it's true. And I had friends who cared.

"I have thought about this for two weeks, running it through my head, trying to organize my thoughts. Allen doesn't know because I wanted you all to hear together.

"I have a plan for the old lodge. I would like to open a mystery weekend for the wealthy. For two or three days at a time. I don't have the particulars now but that will come. After Florence I thought we could create something along those lines. We can modify the lodge to accommodate at least fifty people. We can create games for the wealthy in the lodge and on the grounds. We have all the acreage we need. Similar to the game Clue but on a much larger scale.

"Warren would have to build it. He is the computer guy. That's what he does anyway, but we would all have a say in what should be done. We each have our own skills. We can make good money if done properly. I know rich people and what they need. We, of course, have to challenge them. They bore easily. We are all educated and clever, and I believe we can come up with some wonderful ideas. We show them a great time, and they will spend money and return. We could stay together this way and have our own business. I am not trying to thank you by spending my money, buying you. Everyone is resigning from their jobs. and will be looking for something to do. I can't do this on my own. Contribute as much as you can. You are not obligated to stay if you change your mind. After those two weeks in Italy, we can never go back to our old life. That was exciting and challenging. We couldn't go back to the quiet life. I can't. This could be fun for all of us. What do you think?"

Shelly looked at Warren. "Do you want to move to Germany?"

"Why not. We can sell both houses; that would help."

"Joseph and Luca, you live here; do you want to try this?"

Luca answered, "Yes. We can sell the jewelry store and put that into it. Joseph turned to her. "Are you sure?"

"We can try it, right? I think that it would be good for us."

"Allen, how about you?" Greta was praying.

"I'm in. I have money stashed away. I'll help."

Greta ran up and kissed him. "I love you."

So that was it.

They went to Washington and Warren and Shelly married. Their families and friends were there. Henry and Chris were invited. They enjoyed them-selves but were not happy three of their people resigned and are moving to Germany. They stayed for a week and then flew back to Germany.

They started redesigning the lodge by adding more rooms and a larger kitchen and lobby. Six months later Allen and Greta married. They had a lot to look forward to. They set aside three rooms for the now-married couples. The rest would be for the guests. When someone brought up the mystery weekend, they mentioned Florence as the model.

Warren made the comment, "Yes, but no one will die."